Quinn's

Faith

Diane Garner

thank you

Diane Garner

Published by:
Diane Garner
P.O. Box 1993
Gaylord, Michigan 49734
USA

This is a work of fiction. All persons, places, and
events in this book are fictional.

ISBN-13: 978-1986497008
ISBN-10: 1986497003

Dedication

In memory of my Mama,
Barbara Ellen Hendricks.

You left your strength, love, and selflessness
behind for me to use, and showed the world what
a wonderful woman you were.

I am blessed that God choose you to raise me.

I love you, Mama.

Xoxo

Thanks and Acknowledgements

First and foremost, I would like to thank my editor and friend, Debbie Barry, for all the time and effort she put into helping with my book. She was there to push and encourage me when I needed it most. If it weren't for her, I would still be wondering what's next.

A big thank-you to my sarcastic husband for supporting me. I hope I make it big, so you can retire early. Thanks, Babe.

To my mother-in-law, Wendy Ann Garner, (July 31, 1952 - February 25, 2018), who gave me love, support, and encouragement, not just with my book, but with life in general. You will be greatly missed by everyone who had the pleasure of knowing you the way I did. Until we meet again, may your soul rest in peace.

Thank to Kathy Hockey, an awesome friend and shopping buddy, who always asked for more chapters before they were finished. Because of her, I wrote faster, getting my book done on time.

To Norma Fritz, I want to thank you very much for being a big supporter, and the best neighbor ever.

To Dawn Hendricks, my strong, courageous, and beautiful sister-in-law, for being 100 percent honest with me about my writing. You gave me what I needed to be a better writer, and for that I am thankful.

I would also like to thank iPublishGlobal/ Cover City for the professional and stunning work they did for my book cover and trailer. I look forward to working with you again.

7

Chapter 1

She could feel her heart beating rapidly, painfully, against her ribcage. Panic and fear were starting to set in. The cold – oh my gosh, the cold! The icy water seeped in from every direction. Quinn struggled against the seatbelt, pressed close to her body, making it extremely hard to unbuckle.

"Calm down, calm down, think fast, Quinn!" she said aloud, reaching down into the frigid water to grab onto her submerged bag. Quinn dug around in her bag, until she found her box cutter. Two slashes, and she was free of the belt.

As the Arctic water climbed to her chest, her body felt pain, making it hard to drag air into her lungs. In the distance, Quinn could see a faint glow of light, almost like a flashlight in a dark cave, at a distance.

"Okay. Let's get out of here," she thought. She turned the box knife around, and started beating frantically on the driver side window. With the water rising so high, it wasn't very effective. The window was taking a beating, but not giving in.

The water was too high now. Quinn drew one last breath into her lungs, before being overtaken by the icy water. She kept struggling with the door, hoping that it would just open, because she was willing it to. The glowing light in the water was getting closer and closer, and she was running out of time. The hope of making it out of this was gone. Quinn's chest was starting to burn.

"Why isn't my life flashing before my eyes?" she thought. "I can't hold it any longer." Slowly, her lungs started releasing air on their own; there was no way of stopping it. Quinn was panicking and fighting death for what seemed like forever; the water started painfully filling her lungs, and then the pain started to subside.

"The water doesn't seem so cold now," she thought, as she started to drift off.

The second her eyes closed, she could see a light through her eyelids, and she felt the warmth from the glow. *This must be what heaven is like.* Quinn willed her eyes to open just a tad, and could make out a silhouette.

"An angel to carry me to heaven?"

Out of nowhere, jarring pain shot through the back of her head, and Quinn's eyes flew open. She moaned loudly, gasping as if she'd been holding her breath. After a few seconds of taking in her surroundings, Quinn realized she was in her own bedroom, safe and sound. She'd fallen off the bed, and cracked her head on the hardwood floor. As her breathing returned to normal, relief washed over her.

"It was just a dream," she thought aloud. "I really hate reliving that over and over again. Wasn't once enough?"

Quinn stood up, and looked at the nightstand. The glowing, red digits on her alarm clock read 1:11 am. The cold water from her dream still chilled her veins. She made her way into the bathroom, took the robe off the back of the door, and wrapped herself tightly. She turned to the little, square sink, and placed her hands on each side, then stared at herself in the mirror.

"You need to stop this," she scolded herself aloud.

Every night, for the last month, she'd had the same dream, eating at her, little by little. She just wished she could forget it'd ever happened. These dreams were unlike any dream she'd ever had. She could feel everything she'd felt on the day she'd almost died.

"Is my brain telling me that I shouldn't have lived?"

Quinn listened, as Father David gave his sermon from the front of the church. This was the only place that gave Quinn peace. She looked over at her mom, who had a relaxed, sweet smile on her face, as Father David spoke of forgiveness to all of God's children.

"Quinn!   Quinn!" a voice called.   Quinn looked around, but noticed nothing unusual.   It didn't seem like her mother had heard it, either. She felt a little uneasy.   Quinn stood up, shuffled to the end of the aisle, genuflected, and made the Sign of the Cross, before quietly making her way to the restrooms.   Quinn pushed the door open, and splashed water over her pale face at the sink. Her long, curly, dark hair fell over her shoulder into her face when she bent forward.   Looking into the mirror, she caught coal-black eyes staring back at her.   She blinked quickly, and they were gone.

"Oh, my gosh!   Am I going crazy?" she thought, as she stepped back to the wall.   She leaned her head back against the cold wall, and giggled to herself.   "Black eyes? Really, Quinn! Get a grip!" she whispered to herself.

After Mass, she walked home with her mom: a beautiful lady, with hair graying as it sprawled downward to the middle of her back.   She was a little shorter and thinner than Quinn, but they both had the same big, brown eyes, and full lips. Quinn, however, looked a lot like her dad: well-built, with a tough exterior.   He was a cop, killed in the line of duty before she'd been born.   Her mom talked about him every day, so that Quinn wouldn't feel as though she'd never known him. Quinn had the calm, quiet life that they'd both planned for her.

Quinn and her mom were walking around the corner, near their house, when they were nearly run into by a guy in a white button-down and jeans.

"Oh, my gosh! Are you ladies okay?" the stranger exclaimed, after a quick recovery.

Quinn's mom nodded and said, "We're just fine. What's the rush?"

The guy looked at her with squinting eyes, and said, "I'm only home for a few days, and I asked my mother to make some stuffed peppers and apple pie for dinner. My mom said if I can get there within a half hour, she would."

Quinn's mother nodded lightly, and said, "Well, best get a move on. You're losing time."

The guy looked at Quinn for a second. "Weren't you in church today?"

Quinn had a hard time making eye contact. He seemed brighter than anyone else, and the light hurt her eyes, so she just nodded.

The young man looked back at Quinn's mom, and smiled. "I know you," he said. "You live next door to my mom."

Quinn's mom's eyes opened wide. "Oh! Last time I saw you, Ajax," she tipped her chin down in thought, "you were, what, ten years old?"

Ajax shrugged. "I guess that's about right."

Mom took his hand in hers. "Take yourself back home, and tell your mama you guys'll be joining Quinn and me for dinner, and I'll make sure you get your stuffed peppers."

"Yes, Ma'am. Thank you very much."

They all said their good-byes to one another, and then all headed to their homes.

Once home, Quinn made her way to her bedroom to change out of her church dress. Her bedroom was on the small side, but had its own bathroom connected. She opened the closet, and hung her church dress, and then brought out grey and pink sweatpants with a matching hooded sweater. Even though it was now late spring, she still felt chilled from the accident. After dressing, she went to her bathroom, and washed the makeup off her face. When she looked up, while patting her face dry, the black eyes appeared again. Quinn slowly backed up, and blinked; when she opened her eyes, they were still glaring back. She grabbed the cross around her neck, closed her eyes, and started praying.

Quinn knelt down, and bowed her head. "Living Lord, I'm yours. I wear the helmet of salvation and hope. I carry the shield of faith and your Word. I hold the sword of the Spirit. I buckle the belt of truth around my waist. I put on the breastplate of righteousness, and walk with the boots of readiness and peace. I'm yours. Amen."

Quinn stood on her now-strong legs, and looked into the mirror. The only eyes looking back at her were hers. Quinn walked out of her bathroom, and made a beeline for her bed. Exhaustion hit her fast, and before she could register anything, she was out.

Quinn woke up, startled by the sound of shattering glass. Before she had any time to react, the bedroom door flew open, and in charged her mom, Ajax on her heels, and his mom, Ms. May, right behind him.   The looks on their faces would've been priceless, if this were actually a moment of humor.

"What was that?   Are you okay, Baby?" Quinn's mom asked.

Quinn glanced in the direction of the bathroom.   "I'm fine, Ma.   I think the mirror shattered."

Ajax moved into the bathroom, and then poked his head out. "Yep, that's exactly what happened."   He jerked his head in Quinn's direction.   "Could you grab a broom and dustpan, and we'll get this cleaned up. Mrs. Fellows, Ma, why don't you guys get dinner finished, while we clean this up?"

Quinn left, and came back, wielding a broom and dustpan. "I can't believe it just shattered." she mumbled to no one in particular.

Ajax gave a sarcastic snort. "Wouldn't be the strangest thing that's happened in the last month." The way he said it gave Quinn chills.

They glanced at each other, shrugged, and then continued cleaning up the broken glass.

Quinn stayed quiet throughout a very delicious dinner and friendly discussions.   They chatted about everything, including church, work, favorite television shows, and what Ajax'd been up to.   He seemed to slither around most of the discussion about him.   When the conversation slowed, Quinn offered to do the dishes, and said she'd bring dessert and coffee when she was finished.

Ajax followed the moms into the living room, to catch up on some crime show documentary her mom had been recording. Her ma really loved those shows.

Quinn washed dishes, with soft rock and roll music in the background. There wasn't much to wash; her mom washed while she cooked. While scrubbing the dessert pan, Quinn looked out the kitchen window. It was dark out. She was startled when she noticed movement in the back yard. She looked harder, but saw nothing. She sighed dramatically, and started to rinse the Corningware. Something caught her attention again; she glanced up, and there was the reflection of a face right behind her, looking over her shoulder. Quinn jumped, and the baking dish flew from her grip. A pair of hands caught it in mid-air.

It was Ajax. Quinn turned, badly shaken. "You scared the crap out of me!"

Ajax tried not to smile, but he failed completely. "Sorry; didn't know you were so jumpy. At least I got this," he said, handing her the unharmed dish.

Quinn let out a poof of air. "It's fine. Thank you. It's nothing, just thought I saw…. Never mind." Quinn turned and placed the dish on the rack.

"Saw what?" Ajax asked.

Quinn looked out the window, seeing half of her reflection. "Nothing. Just thought I saw something move right outside the window. I'm sure it's nothing," she said, shrugging her shoulders. "Would you mind taking out the coffee to them? I'll get the pie sliced, and I'll be there in a sec."

Ajax shrugged, and picked up the cups; he left the kitchen.

Quinn turned to the window again. "I can't be going crazy, can I?" she thought.

She wiped her hands on a hand towel, and slipped out the back door to look around. Sure enough, there were footprints outside the kitchen window. Quinn bent down to get a better look. Alongside the prints were what looked like scorch marks.

"What're you doing out here?"

Quinn jumped at the sound of Ajax's voice. "Oh, my gosh! I'm going to put bells around your neck. I swear, you're going to be the death of me!" she whispered loudly.

Ajax smiled, and looked down. The smile vanished when he saw what she was looking at. "Looks like it isn't nothing, after all," he said, nervously, while he guided her by the shoulder back into the house.

Quinn thought he looked a little shook up.

While their moms had coffee and dessert, and watched their show, Ajax and Quinn took theirs to the screened front porch. Quinn made herself comfortable on one end of the sofa, while Ajax plopped down on the other end.

"You don't remember me, do you?" Ajax asked.

Quinn's mouth was full, so she shook her head.

"Wouldn't expect you to. You were, what, two, when I left? I was ten. That makes you what now? Nineteen, right?"

Quinn nodded, and took a sip of her coffee. "Yeah, Mom mentioned you, though. She said she used to babysit while your mom was at work, and she'd do the same for my mom." Quinn paused and took another sip of her coffee. "I'm sorry you got dragged away from your mom. Not saying that it wasn't a good thing or not. I just couldn't fathom what it'd be like not to be with my mom."

Ajax nodded. "I missed her, but she'd come and visit a few times a year. My dad's an ass, but not a jerk. And yeah, I'd prefer to be with my mom. It's good to be back home again."

Quinn finished her last bite of pie. "Why'd it take you so long to come home? You're, what, about 28?"

Ajax put his empty plate aside, and took a long swig of the scalding, black coffee. "Yeah, I'll be 28 next week. I got into business with my dad. Not a good kind, either. Had some issues. He had to fix mistakes I'd made. When he did that, I left." He glanced at his shoes.

Quinn knew he didn't want to talk about it anymore, so she smiled, and said, "Well, welcome home."

Ajax thought it was nice to have someone to talk to: someone who didn't know him, or his past. It was a relaxed conversation. She was so innocent, and had no clue how cruel the world really was.   Back home, the ladies swarmed around him. He had no issues making friends, but not for the right reasons. They thought, if they were close to him, then they'd be safe. It wasn't true.

"Know anywhere that's hiring?" Ajax broke the long silence.

"I work at the factory outside of town. We're always hiring."

"Oh, you work in the office?"

Quinn laughed. "No, I work the floor. An office job'd be nice, but I make more money on the floor, and enough so that Mom doesn't have to work."

"Why didn't you go to college?" Ajax asked.

"Didn't enjoy school, and don't wanna waste the money," she shrugged.   "I worked there throughout high school, under the table, and learned almost everything. I'm good at it. I stick to what I'm good at. Why don't you come to the office tomorrow morning around eight am? I'll let them know you're coming. I get there about 6:30, 6:45, depending on how long it takes to get there."

Ajax chuckled, "The town has traffic now?"

Quinn laughed.   "No, I walk to work.   I totaled my car, and would hate to leave Ma without a car, and plus it's nice out now, and it feels good to get fresh air."

Ajax just shook his head in disbelief, with a crooked smile. "What time do you get out?"

"Seven to 7:30," she responded. "Long days, but short weeks," she added.

Chapter 2

Quinn stood in a field, surrounded by a thin, white mist. The weather was perfect; the field was covered with the most beautiful flowers, and the air was the cleanest she'd ever breathed. Quinn glanced up, and her face was bathed with the warmth of the sun, but when she opened her eyes, there wasn't a sun anywhere. What consumed the sky was nothing but mist, as far as her eyes could see.

She looked down at herself, and everything seemed normal. She was dressed in long, white linen, with a light, lavender rope and tassels holding it together. It reminded her of what she read about the Roman gods. Something about this place made her feel stronger, clearer-minded, and healthier than ever. Suddenly, Ajax appeared in the distance. He still had a glowing essence around him. He was breathtakingly handsome, but appeared to be troubled. Quinn slowly walked toward him. When she was about 20 feet from him, another man appeared behind Ajax, running towards him with a long knife.

Quinn screamed, "No!" and ran. "Stop! Ajax, behind you!"

Quinn was confused, because Ajax didn't seem to hear her. When the man reached Ajax, he stuck the knife into his back, and twisted it; he smiled, and said something that Quinn couldn't make out. In a black poof, the man disappeared, and Ajax fell to his knees. Quinn got to him in time to catch him as he fell back. Tears rolled down her face, mirroring Ajax's, and she could sense his pain and despair. He still didn't even realize she was there.

"What's happening?" Quinn screamed, frustrated at the thought there was nothing she could do.

"There now, Child," a voice said from behind her.

She looked down, and Ajax had vanished from her arms. Quinn looked behind her, and there stood a man, dressed somewhat like her, but with spectacular wings floating at his sides.

"This was but a glimpse into his future; no need to fret just yet."

"Who are you?" Quinn asked, wiping the last of her tears away with the back of her hand.

He was the most beautiful man she'd ever laid eyes on. His eyes were as blue as the sky; his hair was long and golden; his skin was the perfect shade; and his voice was music to the ears. His body was built strong, and perfect in every way.

"I am Michael, and I'm in need of your help."

Quinn's eyes grew wide, and her jaw dropped in shock. "What can I do for you that you couldn't do better?"

Michael closed the gap between them, and placed his hand on her shoulder. "You can help me save Ajax. Bad people are after him, and pure evil is after you. I'll protect you, but our Father needs *you* to protect *him*." He leaned forward, and kissed Quinn's forehead. "My child, our time is up. We will meet again."

Quinn's eyes fluttered open to darkness, still wet from tears she'd shed in her dream. Quinn patted her eyes dry, and looked at the clock; it read three a.m.. She heaved a heavy sigh, still saddened by what she'd witnessed. She'd known Ajax for fewer than 20 hours, but wouldn't wish that horrible death for him. Quinn sat up in bed. "A dream," she thought.

Quinn pulled her belongings out of the locker, and placed her coffee cup inside; she shut and locked it. She'd got to work early, so she was taking off early. She'd kept herself as busy as possible, to keep her mind from floating back to her dream. The dream that kept her up, and the dream that haunted her soul.

Quinn stepped out into the warm, spring evening, and the sky was a light blue, but a little cloudy. She shielded her eyes from the sun, and glanced up. The cloud right above her looked a lot like the angel wings from her dream. Quinn sucked in a shaky breath, and lowered her eyes. When she did, she met Ajax's gaze. He leaned casually against his car, and just smiled, with his hand jammed into his light, faded blue jeans. He wore a white t-shirt, with a blue-and-grey flannel shirt that complemented his blue eyes.

"Hi," Ajax said, taking a step away from his car.

"Hi," Quinn responded, "Did you get the job?"

Ajax nodded. "I did." Ajax took a folded-up paper from his chest pocket. "Here: your mom left you a note. I guess her and Mom are going to some conference about crazy psycho-killers," he said, squinting and shaking his head.

Quinn laughed at the face he was making. She read the note stating where they were going, and that they'd be back in a few days. "They're going to a profiling seminar," Quinn corrected. "You could've given it to me when I got home. You didn't have to drive it all the way here."

Ajax smiled. "Well, I can't boil water to save my life, and I figured cookin'd be the last thing you wanted to do after being on your feet all day. So, I thought, maybe, we could grab dinner."

Quinn narrowed her eyes. "Well, my feet hurt, and I'm starving," she replied.

Ajax opened the passenger side, and she slid in.

Quinn and Ajax went to one of the locally owned restaurants downtown. It was charming, and possibly one of the town's oldest buildings. It was rustic, with a mini cast iron chandelier hanging over each table. The stunning tables were horizontally cut logs, sanded, and cover in clear stain, to show Mother Nature's true beauty.

Ajax and Quinn seated themselves in the back corner of the restaurant, in comfortable silence. It was past dinner time, and the place was quiet, with only a few tables occupied. They scanned the menus, and then set them aside to signal to the wait staff that they'd already chosen what they wanted. The server took their orders, and left them to their own devices.

Ajax cleared his throat. "Find out anything about the footprints outside your window?"

Quinn shook her head. "I'm sure it's nothing. It's the burn marks that bother me most."

Ajax folded his arms in front of him, and leaned back. "That has to be from lighting, or something."

Quinn silently disagreed, with a shake of her head. "Could you take me to the church after dinner?" Quinn knew it sounded odd, and added, "Just wanna visit my dad's grave for a few minutes." He didn't have to know she really needed to talk to Father David about thinking she was going crazy.

"Yeah, not a problem," Ajax said, sitting up straight when he saw the food heading their way. The rest of the meal, they settled for small talk, and she laughed at Ajax's lame, yet funny, jokes.

When Quinn walked into the church, Father David was kneeling in the first pew, with head bowed. Quinn walked up silently, knelt beside him, bowed her head, and prayed. Several minutes passed, and she lifted her head to see that the Father had already taken a seat on the bench.

"Good evening, Quinn. How are you?" Father David sat, relaxed, with his body turned towards Quinn.

Quinn imitated his posture. "I'm unsure of how to answer that question, Father." Quinn paused for a few moments before continuing. "I think I may be going crazy, or something's wrong with me, mentally."

Father David nodded his head slowly. "What makes you think this?"

Quinn rolled her neck; it was getting stiff, so she turned her whole body. "Well, I think evil is after me. I'm not sure if it's real, but I've seen the evil looking back at me."

Father David interrupted. "Is the evil you?"

"No, Father, nothing like that. It's another set of eyes, and everything screams evil. I'm not even sure how to explain it. I think something is wrong with me, Father." The last words shook Quinn enough that tears escaped her eyes.

Father David placed his arm around her shoulders. "I don't believe you're crazy. Ever hear the saying, 'Those who are crazy don't know they're crazy?'" Father David gave a glorious grin at his own humor. "Quinn, I don't believe you're crazy. I've felt a stir in our town, and, until just now, I didn't understand it. I've been praying about it, and my prayers brought you here."

Quinn dried her eyes. "I don't understand, Father."

Father David took his rosary from around his neck, and held it firmly in his hand. "I don't, either, but I'm sure we'll find out soon enough." Father David held the rosary up, and dangled it between him and Quinn. "I want you to take this, and keep it with you at all times."

The rosary was a lot larger than any she'd seen, especially the crucifix.

Father David continued: "If you experience anything again, or feel threatened in any way, shape, or form, use this." Father David flipped open the top of the crucifix, and a spray pump was exposed. "Holy water." Father David flipped the top back on, and placed it around Quinn's neck.

"Thank you, Father, for everything."

Father David rose, and gave Quinn a quick hug. "You're welcome. Keep praying; the Guy Upstairs said it's worked for you in the past."

Quinn's mouth dropped. Father David smiled and walked away.

The ride home was silent, but calm. When Ajax pulled into the driveway, Quinn opened her door, and then turned toward him.

"Want ice cream?"

Ajax stepped out of the car, and shut the door. Quinn followed.

Chapter 3

Quinn was jarred awake by a brutal coughing fit. When she settled her breathing, she noticed she was no longer in her bed. She was lying in filth, and sat on a hard, hot ground that smelled of sulfur. Quinn sat up quickly, and stood up, dusting off her hands. It was so hot, and her breathing was labored; it was painful to drag air into her lungs. She was in the same clothes she'd gone to sleep in: a tank top and underwear. It was dark, but red lights lit the horizon.

"Where am I? Am I dreaming?" she whispered to herself.

Another fit of painful coughing took over, after she spoke. Her mouth was so dry, she had a hard time swallowing, and her throat hurt something horrible. After what seemed like forever, the coughing settled. Quinn turned slowly in circles, but no matter which way she was facing, everything looked exactly the same. Panic started to take root, and Quinn started to whisper a prayer.

"I'm afraid, God. Please lead me in the right direction, and keep me from har..."

A tisking in the distance cut off her prayer. "He cannot help you here, Darling."

The voice let out a thunderous laugh that startled Quinn, making her turn in circles, looking to find where the voice was coming from. In the distance, Quinn saw a very large and handsome man walking gracefully toward her. Quinn was frozen in fear, and had no idea what to do. The man stopped just inches from her face.

"They told me you were fit to be a meal, but they left out how delicious you look."

Quinn held back the bile caused by his rancid breath. "Who are you?"

The man laughed. "I'm Dantanian."

Quinn stepped back. "Stay away from me!"

Dantanian cocked his head to the side. "I can't touch you, yet, Darling. There're things I must put in place before I can do such a thing." He pointed to his eyes and drew his finger across his throat, making the "kill" symbol. "Like dot the Is and cross the Ts. Plus, it's not you I want." He laughed at his own sick humor. "Ajax is mine, and I'll get him. You can't help him; the deal's already been made."

Quinn straightened her back, and stood taller. "You won't have him; his future lies elsewhere. I'll do everything in my power to stop it."

In a flash, Dantanian had her by the neck, his face in hers. "And what power is it that you have, Darling?" The words hissed between his angrily thinned lips. "That's right, stupid, useless human: you lack the power you would need!" He sat her down as though she was a baby. "Child, listen to me. Your oh-so-great father set a fate for you that's cruel. Are you willing to die for this Ajax? Does he mean this much to you? He's a nobody, a criminal, a bad man. How can someone as pure and innocent as you want anything to do with someone like him?"

Quinn didn't back away this time. "I have God on my side, and I'll do what He asks of me. If He's asking me to give my life for someone else, I will."

Dantanian took a step back, and looked extremely irritated. Quinn spread her arms in the shape of a cross as he aimed bolts of lightning at her. Quinn closed her eyes tightly, and showed no fear. When she opened her eyes again, she was safely in her bedroom.

Quinn sat up in bed, and looked at her clock. It was nine in the morning. She heard voices coming from the kitchen. It sounded like Ajax was over for breakfast. Today was Friday, so they didn't have work. She wondered what he was doing there.

Quinn slid out of bed, and noticed that her feet looked like she'd stepped in coal, and she had a scorch mark on the chest of her shirt. She stood up, and tossed it off onto the bed, as if it was on fire. She grabbed some clothing from her closet, and then locked herself in the bathroom to shower the nastiness of the dream from her body. She realized she could still smell his breath.   Quinn shivered, and crawled into the steaming shower.

When Quinn finally emerged from the steamy bathroom, Ajax was sitting on the edge of her bed with the scorched nightshirt in one hand, and ash in his other.

"What's this?" Ajax asked, not looking up.

Quinn leaned back against the door frame, and slid down to sit on the floor. "My dream."

After what seemed like forever, Ajax stood up, held her nightshirt tightly bunched against his forehead, and then placed it back on the bed.

"You must've sleep-walked last night."

Quinn chuckled drily. "Yup, I also walked into a bolt of lightning," she said, sarcastically.

"Quinn, you understand how crazy this sounds, don't you?"

Quinn stood up, and slipped her shoes on, without looking back. "Yes, I do," she said, as she walked out of her room, down the hall, and out the front door.

Chapter 4

"So, Sweetheart, are you going to be okay while I'm away for a couple of weeks?" her mother asked, while pulling weeds from the garden. "We're leaving tonight."

Quinn removed her gloves, and wiped her forehead and eyes with the back of her hand. "I'll be fine, Mom. I'll find something to keep me busy. Just make sure you have tons of fun for the both of us," Quinn replied, with a wink.

"I'm sure Ajax'll be good company, if you get lonely," her mother said sarcastically, while mockingly imitating her wink.

"Mom! You're something else!"

"I could use a nice long vacation," Quinn thought

A little after four in the afternoon, Quinn opened her cell, and noticed she had several missed calls from Ajax. "Huh, guess I should've turned my phone on sooner," she thought to herself. "Oh well, I'll give him a call after Mass."

She opened the door, and, to her surprise, Ajax was sitting in the screened porch.

"What's up?" Quinn asked, as she locked the door.

"Your mom told me you were going to Mass tonight, and, since you've been ignoring my calls, I thought I'd just wait for you."

Quinn placed the keys in her pocket, started out the screen door, and said, "I wasn't ignoring your calls. I was ignoring *all* calls, because I forgot to turn my phone on." Before Ajax could respond, Quinn had already hurried to the sidewalk. It didn't take long for Ajax to catch up to her.

"Wait! Are you pissed at me?"

Quinn didn't flinch at the question. "I don't know you enough to be mad at you about anything. I like time to myself for my thoughts, and not have to explain them to anyone."

Ajax was silent as they walked, until they reached the steps of the church. He gently placed his hands on her shoulder. "Okay."

Quinn looked at Ajax. That simple "Okay" made Quinn smile, and she gave him a nod, before they headed into Mass.

After Mass, Quinn and Ajax sat on a bench at the park, sipping on coffee, across the street from the church. The silence was deafening between them. There weren't many people at the park: a couple on the other side of the park, making out on the bench; a couple with a kid; and a few people walking their dogs. Quinn though it was odd that every dog looked uneasy, doing a lot of barking, and growling. She even heard barking from houses in the distance. They were barking at nothing.

After a while, when the coffee ran out, Ajax turned toward her. "I know weird things've been happening. They've been happening to me, too. I just don't think there's anything supernatural about it. For me, it could be the move back home."

Quinn sat silently for a few moments before she spoke. "Remember me telling you I totaled my car?"

Ajax nodded, but waited for her to continue.

Quinn turned, and folded her feet under her. "I didn't just total the car. The car and I went off the bridge, after the ice started melting from winter." Quinn cleared her throat, and continued. "All my windows were up, and the doors were closed. I wasn't supposed to live."

Ajax rubbed the back of his head. "Rescue crew was fast."

Quinn shivered. "The rescue didn't show up 'til I was already on the shore, out cold. I don't know how I got there. I just remember a light getting bigger, and me letting go. I couldn't hold my breath any longer. I still can't shake the cold from my body." Quinn shivered as she spoke about it.

Ajax took off his jacket, and placed it around her shoulders. "I believe that you believe what you're saying. I don't believe in the unbelievable. I believe in God, but I'm not sure who He is, after the way I was brought up…." Ajax shook his head slowly. "After the way I was brought up, it's hard for me to think God would want a life like that for me, or any kid. I don't believe any of this is super—."

Ajax was cut off when he noticed a sleek-looking man bob his head out from behind a thin, young tree. Quinn noticed, too, and she also noticed that he had a gun in his hand. When the man raised his gun, to shoot, another man, more vaguely outlined, suddenly appeared beside him. The second man was a sleek, handsome, and confident man.

Quinn whispered, "Dantanian."

Dantanian ignored the gunman. Dantanian raised his hand, and sent a bolt of blue and white lightning right at Quinn and Ajax. Moving with the speed of reflex, Ajax pushed Quinn off the bench, with force that landed her roughly on the ground, with his body sprawled protectively over hers. It made her ears ring. Their bodies froze as they heard glass shattering very near them.

Then everything went eerily silent. Even the dogs were silent. The silence only lasted a second or two, before people start talking excitedly. Quinn and Ajax looked up, and both the gunman and Dantanian were gone.

Ajax sat up, pulling Quinn with him. Quinn could hear the whispers.

"Freaky lighting."
"Where'd that come from?"
"Oh my God!"

Then a scream erupted from a few feet behind them. A woman stood by the lamp post, stiff as a board. "My baby!", she screamed, as her husband pulled her tight against him.

Everything seemed fuzzy to Quinn. She looked behind the bench, where people were pointing. The bench where *she* had been sitting! The glass from the exploded street lamp was shattered, and, about five feet behind the bench, a girl about 10 years old, was lying on the grass, with a triangular piece of glass sticking out of her chest. Blood was pooling around her. She was very still, her eyes closed, as if she was sleeping soundly, but her body was lifeless. Her beautiful, long, blonde hair was tinged with red from the blood.

Ajax jumped up, and yelled, "Someone call for help!" Then, he went to her, and felt for a pulse.

When his head dropped, Quinn couldn't hold back the tears. She sat there, trying to comprehend the scene around her. Quinn crawled to the innocent girl's body, and placed her hand on the girl's head. She prayed, and cried, until Ajax pulled her to her feet, and walked her away, when the medics arrived.

Even though Quinn was out of it, she could hear everything around her in normal tones, but people were moving in slow motion. She heard one of the couples tell a cop that it was a bolt of lightning. The couple with the child saw the same bolt of lightning, as well. Others weren't sure what happened.

"It happened so fast, but my dogs were acting funny, so we were just leaving the park."

When the sun was going down, and all the people and the commotion left, Quinn was still sitting there, on the ground, near the bench, where it all started. Quinn looked down at her blood-stained hands, which were shaking uncontrollably. Her eyes were blurry, and her face was tear-streaked and swollen. Her mind felt numb, and she was having trouble thinking clearly. Quinn's thoughts were either flowing fast, or they weren't making any sense. Everything seemed to become a jumbled mess.

"We should start heading home, okay?"

Quinn looked to her left. Ajax was kneeling beside her, and looking at her, concern in his eyes. She had no clue how long he'd been there.

Quinn nodded, "Okay. I'm okay." She whispered, afraid her voice would fail her.

Ajax took her hand, and helped her up.

The water fell from the shower head with force. The only thing that relaxed Quinn wasn't working this time. She was cold and achy. She kept replaying everything in her head. Could she have stopped Dantanian, or saved the child's life? What made her feel worse was that she knew it was meant for her or Ajax. Why did she freeze?

Quinn shut off the water, stepped out of the tub and wrapped her robe tightly around her. She leaned back against the bathroom wall, and slid down the wall to the floor. Her body shook from the silent, painful sobs that took control of her.

When Ajax came back to her house, he found her up against the bathroom wall, in her bathrobe. She was crying uncontrollably, with her head in her hands. He stood there, not sure what to do. She was so upset, she didn't even notice him there. His first though was to leave, but he couldn't just leave her there. He knew how she felt.

Ajax sat on the floor beside her, and pulled her into a hug, letting her cry into his chest. She smelled of honey and lavender. Her scent soothed him; he wished it did the same for her.

After a while, Quinn settled down, but made no effort to move. She found comfort after he sat with her. Ajax smelled of the woods. His scent was relaxing. It relaxed her enough that her insides stopped shaking, and exhaustion crept in. Quinn just sat there, listening to his heartbeat, ,as she fell fast asleep.

Chapter 5

The dark of night crept in, and the moon cast dancing shadows on Quinn's bedroom wall. The house was still and silent. The only sound was the branches and leaves rustling in the breeze outside the bedroom window, and the faint ticking of the clock at the end of the hall.

Ajax looked down on of the girl lying against him. At the moment, Quinn looked so peaceful. He hated seeing her in so much emotional distress. His heart told him that she should be shielded from things like these. Then he thought of his own past.

"Could I have turned into someone who would put people like Quinn through hell? Has anything I ever done made someone feel like she did a half hour ago?" Ajax felt a pang of guilt. "I've done some bad things, but nothing to bring harm to anyone. I couldn't live with myself if I did," he thought.

His mind went back to the last night he'd seen his dad: the night he left. His dad had sent Ajax on one of his "errands;" he'd said it would be in and out. It'd been far from what Ajax's father had promised.

When Ajax arrived at the location, it was a little cottage-like home, which was overrun with weeds. He could see a child sitting by the window, with a woman, eating a meal. Ajax knew this was odd. A few moments later, a text from his father confirmed his suspicions.

The test read: "The man who used to live there owed me money. I want you to collect from his wife. If they don't have it, there is something to take care of this issue in the glove compartment."

Ajax opened the glove compartment. Lo and behold, there was a pistol.

Ajax didn't have to think about it. There was no way he would do something like this. So, he sealed the gun and the cell phone, with all of the information it held, in a box, along with a letter explaining everything, and then left it at the local police department.

He left town. After a few months of driving around, he landed at his mom's house. He knew that it wasn't the best idea, but he couldn't keep running.

Ajax felt completely, physically and emotionally, drained, as he emerged from the memory. He didn't remember ever feeling like that before, in his entire life. His arm still held Quinn tightly to him, and his head leaned back against the wall. The weight of the day's events pulled him down, and a tear escaped his eyes, but he brushed it away before it even had a chance to fall.

"That poor little girl. I never wanna see anything like that again, for as long as I live," he thought to himself. His thoughts were with her family. Their lives would never be the same. Thinking about the day made him simmer with anger.

"What the hell is going on?" he whispered with frustration. If it hadn't been for Quinn, sleeping in his arms, he might have put his fist through the wall. His head felt as though it was on fire, from all of his thoughts.

"That guy with the gun looks like someone I've seen before," his thoughts continued. Could he've worked with my dad? Did me leavin' piss my own father off this much? The other dude seemed to be interested in Quinn. Why would anyone want to harm her? What could she've done to make someone mad at her? Could what she's been tellin' me be true?" he wondered. "No, this's just too crazy. If it's true, I need to find out what's going on."

After Ajax'd been brainstorming against the bathroom wall for a while, with Quinn against his chest, she seemed to be sleeping soundly, but looked a little uncomfortable. He lifted her as gently as possible, walked into her bedroom, and laid her down on her bed. He covered her with a blanket he found folded at the end of the bed. After he made sure she was warm, and sleeping quietly, he walked through the house, to make sure all the windows and doors were shut and locked. After securing the new window over the kitchen sink, he poured himself a tall glass of water, and guzzled it. He hadn't realized how thirsty he was, until he followed it with another glass.

"I definitely need a shower," he thought to himself. He didn't feel right about leaving Quinn by herself, so he grabbed his night pants out of his duffel bag, which he'd left at her house the last time he was there, and went back to the bathroom.

The short shower was relaxing but made Ajax feel even more tired than he'd already been. When he dried off, and dress for the night, in his pajama bottoms, he crumpled up his bloodied shirt, and tossed it in the bathroom trash bin; he silently left the bathroom, took the extra pillow from Quinn's bed, and made himself comfortable on the small recliner, next to the bed. Her scent was all over the chair.

"She must sit and read, or something, in it," he mused. "I wonder what she enjoys reading." He leaned back in the chair, stretching, and let out a little moan, as his body relaxed a little. He turned his face toward Quinn, yawned silently, and fell fast asleep.

Chapter 6

When Quinn woke, she wasn't in her own bed, but a bed as soft as the clouds. She'd never felt material like this before. It was something only angels would sleep on. Quinn stretched out and yawned. After a few minutes of enjoying the bed, she sat up. To her amazement, this place just got prettier. Above, below, and in every direction, was the greenest grass she'd ever seen, and white, fluffy clouds, as well. This time, there weren't any flowers, just the vibrant green grass. From all directions, she could hear the sounds of birds. It was a heavenly sound, and relaxing, too.

Quinn stood up. Again, she was dressed in a long, white, pretty robe, with a rope belt and tussles. "Hello," She called out. "Is anyone here?"

When no one called back, Quinn strode across the grass, enjoying the feel of each blade of grass softly touching her feet, bringing her senses alive. This place even smelled of heaven. At least, it was what Quinn though heaven would smell like. "If I could bottle this scent," she said, giggling.

"You would be popular, in deed," a strong and musical voice said, behind her.

Before Quinn even turned, she knew it was Michael. He was dressed the same way he'd been the last time she'd seen him, in a robe like hers, with floating wings.

"Why am I here now?" Quinn asked, innocently.

"You are our hope. Do you remember everything I told you last time we spoke?" he asked. "Not the time we met here, but at the accident," he added.

Quinn looked a little confused.

"Don't worry yourself, Quinn, it will all come back to you when the information is needed. Then you can take the information, and do as you will with it."

"What does that mean?" Quinn asked, squishing her brows together.

"Trust me, Child, you will understand soon enough."

Quinn gave up on that subject when all the memories came flooding back from the park, and a single tear rolled down her face.

"Quinn, there's nothing you could have done. No one could have stopped it, and the child was the real target, because they wanted you to back off. You couldn't have changed the outcome."

"They killed a child because of me?" she asked, not to anyone specific. "Why did I even go to Mass yesterday?" she thought to herself.

"Because you needed God and his guidance."

Quinn nodded, and then thought to herself, "You can hear my thoughts?"

"Only the ones you allow me," Michael said.

Silently, then, the two walked in the gorgeous fields. There were animals that she hadn't noticed the last time she'd been there. A stunning doe bounced from the bushes. The doe stopped, and then walked closer, and held no fear in her eyes. Quinn held out her hand, and the doe nudged her. She stood there, and let Quinn pet her for a couple of minutes, before she gracefully pranced off.

"What a glorious moment," Quinn thought.

"This place is off-the-wall beautiful. There's nowhere in the world as beautiful as this. I can't imagine never seeing this place again, or feeling the peace and comfort it provides. It feels like home. It makes it all too easy to forget about everything and everyone."

Just as she thought that, Quinn started to get drowsy, and fell down. She felt no pain from falling. She just fell slowly and softly, but never reached the ground.

Chapter 7

When Quinn's eyes opened, she was met by a beautiful sight: a simple peacefulness. Her tired eyes rested upon a stunning creature, one of God's perfectly imperfect creations. The glow that she'd seen around Ajax since he'd got back to town was brighter than usual, maybe because ...

"His soul is at peace when he is in a state of slumber," she realized.

Ajax's eyes were lightly closed, just barely moving under the lids. His Adam's apple bobbed when he swallowed from time to time, and his powerful chest rose and fell with every gentle breath he took. At that moment, Quinn knew that this man had to have a clean soul. She smiled to herself when she realized she cared for him. God had placed Ajax in her path for a reason. "Whatever reason, God, I'll follow where you lead me. Thank you," she whispered.

After a while of enjoying the sight of God's fantastic creation, she realized she ought to get up and dressed before he woke up. Quinn changed quickly and quietly into a pair of stretchy black shorts and a cami that read, "I am His daughter," and showed a pointer finger pointing to the heavens. She combed out her long, dark hair, and tossed it up in a loose bun on the top of her head.

She tiptoed her way to the kitchen. From the hall, she could smell the aroma of the coffee that had already been brewed.

Quinn grabbed a mug, filled it, and sat Indian-style on a chair at the kitchen table.

Quinn snagged her phone from the middle of the table, took a long, soothing sip of her coffee, and opened the phone. She texted her mom.

"Hi, mom. I hope u r enjoying your vacation. Not sure if you'd heard, but last night I watched a freak accident happen. A little girl in the park was killed by a shard of glass. They are saying it was a bolt of lightning that caused it. It was a painful evening mom......" She hit *Send*.

"I just wanted to let you know, I am alright, so you wouldn't worry." *Send* again.

"Ps. Thank you for setting the alarm on the coffee pot before you left."

Quinn pushed *send*, and sat back, sipping her coffee. "Lighting, my butt!" she thought, but she would never tell her mom what she knew happened.

Not five minutes later, Quinn's phone chirped under her fingertips. It was a text message from her mom.

"Hi, my baby girl. I was just on the phone with the church's secretary, and she told me all about it. I was going to text you as soon as she hung up. That poor girl and her parents! I wouldn't know what I would do if I was her mother. It's devastating. Pray a long prayer with me today, Baby; maybe it will bring some comfort to the parents in their time of need."

The phone chirped again. "I am so sorry you had to witness such a tragedy. With everything going on, I would feel better if you had Ajax over for company."

It chirped again as she finished reading. "You are welcome for the coffee."

Quinn refilled her mug, and sat down to respond to the texts.

"Ajax was there when it happened, and he hasn't left. You were right, he is good company. I think I will lie low today, maybe invite Father David over for dinner. I love you, Mom. Xoxo"

Not a minute passed before her mom responded. "Good, you do that! I love you too, Baby Girl. XOXO"

Quinn smiled and set her phone down. At that same moment, she heard a not-so-dexterous sound of bare feet making slapping sounds on the hardwood floor. Quinn went and filled another mug just as Ajax entered the kitchen. He stretched and made a growling noise. He was still shirtless, and his eyes were just slits in his handsome face. Quinn handed him the cup of coffee, and Ajax smiled and grunted something along the line of "Thank you."

In silence, Quinn cooked a quick breakfast. Ajax tried to help by cracking eggs, but he failed miserably, and they ended up digging shells from the bowl.   She couldn't help but laugh as he playfully acted frustrated.

"Thank you for breakfast," Ajax said, while drying the last dish.

Quinn raised an eyebrow and gave a cocky, sideways smile. "Welcome. Thanks for the help," Quinn replied.

Ajax grinned. "I can see the sarcasm seeping off you today!" He scrunched up the dish towel, wound it up, and released it on the back of her thigh.

Quinn let out a yelp, followed by a fit of laughter. She took a few steps in his direction, and raised her chin just enough to look into his eyes.   She could tell he was tensing up by the tightening of the muscles in his shoulders.   "I don't get mad, Ajax, I get even," she said, trying to keep a straight face; she failed.

Ajax's face split into an evil grin, and he winked. "Good, it gives me something to look forward to."

Quinn took a deep breath, smiled, and shook her head.

"Hey, on a serious note, I'm inviting Father David over for dinner tonight, and I wanted you to be…." Quinn stumbled on her words. "I mean, I'd like it if you'd join us for dinner." Quinn's face burned with embarrassment, and she glanced down, fiddling with her fingers.

Ajax smiled.   He wanted to tease her about blushing, but he refrained from doing so. " Yeah, that actually sounds great! You wouldn't want me wasting away." Ajax paused for a moment, looking down at himself with a lopsided grin. "Although, I really should go home and find some real clothes."

Quinn nodded and smiled.

"You gonna be alright for a while on your own?" Ajax asked, turning to walk to the door.

Quinn followed, still a bit on the red side. "I'll be fine," she said with a tight smile.

After Ajax left, Quinn ran to her room. She made her bed and brushed her teeth. As she was putting away her toothbrush, she noticed Ajax's bloody shirt in the trash. She kneeled down, and removed the trash bag. It was a significant amount of blood. No wonder he'd thrown it away. A tear escaped her eyes, but she quickly brushed it away.

"Not today, Satan, not gonna get me today!" she whispers aloud.

Quinn busied herself in the kitchen for a large part of the afternoon. She patted out some burgers, and took buns and Polish sausage out to defrost. She prepared pasta salad and three-bean salad, and put them in the fridge to cool. She sliced onions and tomatoes for the burgers. She also took an apple pie that her and her mom premade out of the freezer.

After she was done prepping the food, she called Father David, and he was happy to be invited. Quinn told him he could come around seven.

By the time everything was done, and the kitchen cleaned up, Quinn was exhausted. She lay down on the couch, out on the screened-in porch. It was cool today, like a storm would be moving in. Quinn laid her head on a fluffy pillow, and pulled her mom's handmade quilt over her. Her body went limp as she relaxed, and her consciousness slipped away.

Chapter 8

Quinn's eyes flew open in panic, as water invaded her lungs. It was painful.

Then her eyes drifted closed, and she felt warmth envelope her body. Water disappeared from her lungs, and was replaced with oxygen.

Quinn slowly opened her eyes, and saw a man surrounded with heavenly light. He smiled, and held her close. She was still under water, but she was warm and dry, and she could breathe. She could hear his thoughts.

"God needs you, my child. God needs you to save...."

"Quinn!" Ajax's voice startled Quinn awake.

She opened her eyes. Ajax was kneeling beside the couch, with his face close to hers.

"You okay?" he asked.

Quinn, still a little dazed, sat up slowly, and nodded. "Yeah, I guess I was just tired. You doing alright?"

"Yeah," he said, drawing out the word. "I'm good." He stood up. "What can I help you with, before Father gets here?"

Quinn stretched and stood up. "Not much; everything's ready. All that's left to do is put the meat on the grill."

Quinn was no more than three feet from Ajax. She could smell the Ivory soap. He was freshly dressed in dark dress pants and a black V-neck t-shirt. His hair was still wet from the shower, and combed back. Quinn smiled. "Are you dressed up?"

Ajax smoothed the front of his shirt, looking a little satisfied with himself. " Father David's coming; felt like I should dress as if I'm going to church."

Quinn quirked her brow. "You look great."

Ajax slowly started walking into the house. "I'm happy you think so. I didn't just dress up for Father David, y'know."

Quinn laughed, and playfully shoved him through the front door.

Ajax laughed lightly. "Hey, take it easy on the scrubs, Babe. Don't go makin' me wrinkled."

Everything was ready out on the back patio when Father David arrived. He was dressed down, in a short-sleeved, flannel, button-down shirt and worn jeans. His somewhat long, salt-and-peppered hair was pulled back. His long stubble beard and mustache were neat and clean, as always. Without his priestly attire, no one would ever know he was a priest. Father David was in his late forties, with the build of a hard labor worker. He stood just under six feet tall, and was about two hundred pounds. He was the sweetest man, and the most popular priest. It seemed like attendance at Mass had tripled since he'd been assigned to the church.

"Ajax, man, how've you been?" Father David asked, patting Ajax on the shoulder. "Why're you dressed up? Got a date tonight?"

Quinn walked in, smiling, and raised an eyebrow at Ajax. Ajax laughed and winked at Quinn.

"No, Father," Ajax said. "I dressed for you," he added as serious as he could.

Father David laughed heartily.

All three of them chit-chatted over dinner. The men each enjoyed a nice, cold beer, and Quinn drank water with her dinner. After dinner was over, there was nothing left over. The men had eaten like they'd been deprived for days. Quinn enjoyed their company, but not as much as she enjoyed watching them enjoy their meal.

Everything was going well until the rain started pelting out of the sky, as though the heavens had opened up and sent a flood. All three grabbed what they could, and ran inside as fast as they could. Luckily, they didn't get too soaked.

Quinn sent the guys into the living room, while she put on a pot of coffee and did what few dishes she had. She'd used the "fine china" tonight: paper plates and red Solo cups. She removed the apple pie from the fridge, and sliced it up.

After waiting for the coffee to finish, Quinn put everything on a wooden serving tray and made her way to the living room. She didn't bother leaving the unserved part of the pie in the kitchen. She heard a serious conversation going on, so she entered as quietly as she could. Ajax was telling Father David something about his father. She overheard something about turning his father in and leaving. Quinn felt odd, and uncomfortable about eavesdropping; she put the tray of coffee and pie down on the coffee table, and headed back to the kitchen, pretending to busy herself by wiping down the counters and drying out the sink.

When Quinn finished, she looked up out the kitchen window. The rain seemed to be slowing down. She looked away for a second, hanging the dish rag, and then looked back at the window. Ajax's reflection was behind her, standing in the doorway, leaning against the frame, with his head cocked to the side. His expression was gentle.

"I wanted you to hear that. If you like, I can fill you in later. Come and join us now?"

Quinn turned, smiled, and wiped her hands on her shorts. She nodded, and Ajax moved aside just enough so she could get by. He followed her back to the living room.

Once everyone was seated, Father David brought up the incident involving the little girl, from the night before. Quinn's gut twisted; she placed her uneaten pie on the coffee table, and took a sip of the coffee she'd poured herself a few moments before. The liquid scalded her mouth, but it was pleasant compared to the pain she felt for that little girl. Even though she knew it was not her fault, she couldn't help but feel the guilt eating at her. Something nagging at her, and eating her from the inside out. She had a good idea who that was. The Devil himself.

Father David cleared his throat, startling Quinn out of her thoughts.

"Are you alright? You look a little pale, Quinn," Father David said with a look of worry.

"Yeah, I think I'm alright. I just don't wanna talk about it right now, Father."

Father David smiled sweetly and nodded his head. "I understand, Child. If you ever need to talk...." Before he could finish his thought, a clap of thunder startled them all, and the rain fell from the sky fast and hard.

Father David shook it off, and laughed at himself. "Okay, kids, I think that's my cue to head home."

Everyone laughed. Quinn stood up and got Father David an extra umbrella from the hall closet, so he wouldn't get drenched on the way to his car.

"Thanks for coming to dinner tonight, Father. It's always great to have you over."

Father David gave Quinn a loving hug. "No, thank you for having me over. I've never had a bad meal here, that's for sure."

Father David shook Ajax's hand, opened the umbrella, and left, waving as he got into his car.

"Drive safe!" Ajax yelled.

"Let's finish our coffee," Ajax said, putting his arm lightly around Quinn's shoulders, and walking them back to the loveseat.

They both sat down and refilled their mugs. Quinn could see his jaw muscles tensing, then relaxing. She watched as he ruffled up his hair, as if he was nervous. Quinn wanted to say something, but wasn't sure whether she should.

After a long few minutes Ajax spoke. "I learned, after a couple of years living with my dad, that he was a criminal. He lived with, ate with, slept with, bargained with, and surrounded himself with criminals. He loaned money out, and asked for it back with an incredibly high interest. Mostly to those who were desperate. I truthfully didn't know how bad it was. When I turned 16, I started working for him. I collected from bookies and businessmen, who always paid their debts. This is what I thought my dad's business was. No, it was much worse than I'd thought."

Quinn listens without interrupting. He had tons of guilt, and maybe a little fear, written all over his face. She knew he would get to the worst part soon enough. She warmed up their coffee, as he took a minute to reflect on what he was going to say next. She put a comforting hand on his arm as he continued.

"One day, he sent me on what he said would be an easy and quick run. This is when I learned how cruel he was. He had me park out at a house. All I could see through the window was a woman and a child. I guess she was a recent widow, or something. I don't know all the facts. Anywho, he gave me an envelope to open when I arrived. Had a note in it that said something along the lines of, 'If they can't pay, use force,' and there was a gun in the glove compartment."

Ajax looked into Quinn's eyes. To his surprise, she wasn't judging him. Her eyes were soft and understanding. The hand she had on his arm gave him a squeeze, letting him know it was okay to continue.

"Well, I didn't. I couldn't do what he wanted. I knocked on her door, and left a huge stack of money that I'd collected for my father. I left it with her, so she wouldn't have to worry for a while, at least. After that, I dropped off the envelope, with the letter and everything, at the police station. Let them know where I was gonna be when, and if, they ever were to do anything with my dad. I drove around for a long time, and landed back here, with mom. Probably not the best thing to do, right? Me coming here could be a bad thing for everyone that I know."

Quinn had slid her hand down to his. "You did what you had to do. Whatever happens here'll be no one's fault but your father's. I'm happy you're here, even if you're dragging trouble with you." Quinn giggled after she spoke the last words.

Ajax was a little set back at her reaction, so much that he didn't laugh with her. He'd thought she would be a little freaked out, or would even, maybe, make him leave. Ajax was in awe of the woman facing him.

He reached up, and ran his thumb down her cheek. He noticed she froze, but her expression never changed. He went back and did it again. This time, she leaned into his touch.

Quinn was a little shocked when Ajax caressed her face. He'd looked a little put off by her just a second before. "Maybe that's not what he's feeling at all," she thought.

They said nothing. He was holding one hand, and the other was on her cheek. Nothing felt wrong. Everything, for one moment, felt right.

Ajax leaned in, placed a small kiss on her forehead, and one on her cheek. He focused his eyes on hers. They seemed to be in a trance with each other. Their faces were just inches apart.

They stayed that way for a long moment before Quinn raised her hand and placed it on the side of his face. This action made Ajax close his eyes for a split second.

Quinn leaned in, and pecked the corner of his lips. His lips turned up into a small smile. Their lips were so close. They could almost taste the apple pie that lingered on them.

Chapter 9

As soon as their lips connected, the lights went out, and the only thing that lit the room was a flash of lighting. Everything went quiet enough to hear the beat of their own hearts. Quinn and Ajax jumped to a standing position. It wasn't the power outage or the lightning that scared them. It was the face looking in the window when the lightning struck; it had illuminated the face. Ajax grabbed Quinn's arm, and yanked her forcefully out of the living room and down the hall, and pushed her into her room.

He pointed his finger at her and said sternly, "Lock the door!"

Quinn didn't know how to respond, so, when Ajax shut the door, leaving her alone inside, she locked it, and then ran over to the phone, and picked up the receiver. She was thankful it wasn't a hand-held. Quinn dialed 911, but there was no dial tone. Nothing.

"Lines must be down," she thought.

"Come on," she said, aggravated.

Quinn rubbed her hands on her pants pocket to locate her cell phone. It wasn't there.

"Oh, come on!" she whispered loudly.

Now she was shaking. "I left it on the kitchen table," she thought to herself.

Quinn ran over to the bag that she used for work, and grabbed a box knife. "I need to get to my phone," she thought. When Quinn reached to unlock the door, her bedroom window shattered. A little in shock, Quinn didn't move at first, until she saw someone already halfway inside her room. That was when Quinn's adrenaline took hold. She turned toward her bathroom, and ran. Right when she had the door closed, but before she could lock it, the door burst open, sending her flying into her glass shower door. She hit so hard that it cracked. Stunned and disoriented, she slipped to the floor. Her head throbbed from the impact. She shook her head to clear her vision, but just then she felt her foot being picked up. Quinn could see the back of a person in a black suit. He yanked her foot, and she smacked her head on the floor. Quinn groaned in anguish. As he dragged her, she saw her box cutter, so she twisted around and grabbed it. The man was impatient, and he yanked her harder for a few steps, until he reached her room. Quinn quickly hid the box cutter in her pocket.

"Who are you? What do you want?" she demanded, still on her back. The intruder was looking at his phone.

So, she said it again. She knew he was going to get aggravated, and that was what she was looking forward to.

"Hey! I asked you a question!" she screamed annoyingly.

She saw that scream get to him. So she did it again, rolling over to her side, thinking she would try to stand. Just as she was in the midst of screaming, he moved fast, and kicked her in the ribs, sending her rolling and coughing, trying to catch her breath. She gained some control, and then she quietly stood up. She had her box knife in her palm, her head turned to look behind her.

"Sit down!" the man said angrily. "Never said you can move."

Quinn stood still, and didn't reply. The guy stepped forward with intent, and grabbed the hair on the back of her head; he brought her face close to his.

"If you want to live through this, you'll listen, you imbecile!" He yanked her head back, so that her eyes faced the ceiling fan. The guy cleared his throat, and then grabbed her waist with the other hand. "Or maybe you should keep acting up; trust me, nothing excites me more. Maybe this'll make Ajax mad enough to face his dad," he said, as he slid his hand slowly down her back.

"You don't want to do this!" Quinn's voice quivered.

"Oh, I do. I'm not too worried about Ajax. He's a coward!" he growled.

Quinn could feel the heat of his breath on her bare neck.

"No, you don't have to worry about him at the moment," Quinn whispered, as she turned her hand around, pushed the blade out as far as it would go, and jabbed it in his side, just under his arm. He grunted in pain, and fell to his knees. Quinn tried to make a run for it, but he grabbed her ankle, making her face plant on the hardwood floor. Her adrenaline was pumping, and she didn't bat an eye at the blood running from her nose and busted lip. When she realized he still had her ankle, she used the other foot to kick him in the face with every ounce of force she had left. He let go. Once released, she was on her feet and out her bedroom door.

Quinn made her way to her mother's room, and shut and locked the door behind her. She swung open the closet door, put in a code on the security pad of a large locker, and grabbed her father's Smith and Wesson. She pulled it out, and looked it over. Her father's 1989 S&W was a six-shot single-action revolver. Her mother had told her that her dad called it his beautiful beast. Quinn understood why. The frame, cylinder and barrel were stainless steel, and clean as a whistle; the grip was a dark but worn wood. After she'd loaded it, she put her hand on the grip, safety still on. Her hand seemed to sink right into her father's imprint. Quinn took a deep, shaky breath. She'd only used this gun when she was doing gun safety classes. With the safety on, she took a minute to breathe before she decided to leave the safety of the bedroom.

Quinn calmed herself, and headed to the door. Just as she was about to grab the knob, someone started banging on the bedroom door. She froze.

"Quinn, are you in there? Are you alright?" His voice sounded hysterical.

Quinn tucked the gun quickly into the back of her jeans. She turned the doorknob, and just fell into Ajax. His shirt was drenched, but she didn't care.

"Oh my God, Quinn, are you okay?" He lifted her face. "Quinn, you're bleeding."

She pulled back, and leaned on the door frame. "I think I'm okay," she said, looking down at the blood on her shirt.

"What happened to you?" Ajax asked.

"Someone broke into my bedroom window. It wasn't the same guy we saw out the window." Quinn sucked in a deep breath. "I stabbed him; he may still be in my room," she said in a shaky breath.

Ajax raised his fingers to his lips and whispered, "Stay here."

Quinn shook her head, and poked it out to watch as he headed down to her bedroom.

Ajax walked slowly toward Quinn's bedroom. The door was slightly ajar, with bloody handprints on the door and door jamb. He pushed the door open with one hand, and the scene unfolded before him. Not far from the door, blood was smeared on the hardwood floor. About five feet from that was a large about of blood. The room seemed empty. The bathroom door was wide open, cracked and partially unhinged. As he approached the bathroom, he noticed that the shower door was cracked, with what looked like a head imprint. He moved closer, and he realized there was hair stuck on the outside of the shower door.

"Quinn needs to see a doctor," he thought to himself.

Ajax took care not to touch anything as he left the room to call the cops.

After he hung up with the police, he went back to check on Quinn. He peeked in from the

hallway to find her clutching the gun. Ajax
stepped into the room, and walked over to her.

"Can we put this away? The cops are on their
way here."

Quinn looked up. "Um. Uh. Okay," she said,
nodding her head.

Quinn walked to the safe, and put the gun in
its rightful place.

Ajax walked over and put his arms around her
shoulders, and Quinn automatically leaned into
him. He could tell that she was exhausted,
whether it was from the struggle, a concussion, or
both.

"Let's go out to the porch and wait. We're
gonna have the paramedics take a look at you."

Ajax guided her from the room, and onto the
porch.

Not long after Ajax made the call, the cops and
EMS arrived. Ajax took the head detective
through the house, and told him everything he
could. In the back of the ambulance, Quinn gave
her statement to an officer, as she was getting
looked at. The time seemed to drag by for Quinn.
Everything seemed quiet for moments, and then
the sound would come in loud and crackly. Kind
of like a broken set of speakers.

"Ma'am, can you lay back, so I can check your
ribs?" the paramedic asked with a soft smile.

Quinn laid back, and the parametric felt
around. Quinn groaned when he hit the ribs that'd
been kicked less than twenty minutes before.

"Okay, looks like you may have a couple
bruised ribs, a cracked rib, and a minor

concussion. I'd like to take you to the hospital," the parametric said, as he helped her sit up.

"No," was all Quinn said.

"Fine," the paramedic said reluctantly. "I need you to sign this, though," he added, pulling out a clipboard with a form on it, and handing her a pen.

Quinn signed the form without reading it, and handed it back.

"I think you should be okay; just make sure you follow up with your doctor as soon as you can, the paramedic told her. "If anything gets worse, you have any issue breathing, or vision troubles, please head to the ER. We don't take concussions lightly anymore."

Quinn nodded, and Ajax finished his statement. The detective thanked him for making sure the files were sent over from the other department, where he'd reported his father. He then went and waited behind the big red and white rig, as they finished up with Quinn. He overheard everything about her medical state. He was so peeved that he was shaking inside.

"How can a grown man beat up on a woman?" he thought, as he cringed. Ajax took a deep breath, and let it out. When he saw Quinn about to exit the rig, he stepped up, and made her sit down to get off.

"Don't need you any more broken than you already are," he whispered under his breath, enough, he hoped, so she wouldn't hear.

"I'm gonna be fine," she replied.

"Ajax! Quinn!"

They both looked over to the detective as he was closing in on them.

"Do you guys have somewhere else to go?" he asked in a hushed voice.

Quinn and Ajax looked at each other.

"My mom's place right here," Ajax said, squinting his eyes.

The detective shook his head, and opened his little notebook.

"You don't understand, son.   Multiple men from your dad's circle are now in town. Meaning that they are here, or heading here. So you can't be here. For y'all's own safety."

The detective paused, and rocked on his heels like he was contemplating how to say his next words.

"We could put you in protective custody, but I think that would be a bad idea. Your dad has someone on the inside."

Everyone fell silent for a moment.

"I have a place you can stay."

It was the voice of Father David. He was coming up from behind Quinn and Ajax.

"Go pack the things you'll need for a long weekend getaway, while the detective and I have a chat. Oh, and leave your cell phones behind."

Quinn and Ajax didn't split ways. They helped each other pack what was needed for wherever it was they were going. Before Quinn left her house, she packed a cooler with a couple days' worth of fast, easy foods, drinks, and snacks. She also grabbed her handy first aid kit, and tossed it on top. While Ajax took the cooler to the door, Quinn took the unloaded handgun from her father's safe and placed it in her almost empty purse, along with a small box of ammunition. It wasn't long before they had everything they needed crammed into one huge duffel bag, and were ready for whatever was about to happen next.

Father David was sitting on the porch, waiting for them. He looked at Quinn, and handed her a large envelope.

"Don't open this till you're on the road. Everything you'll need is in there. The only ones who know what's inside this are the detective and myself. Don't use your bank or credit card."

Father David handed a set of keys to Ajax.

"Here, take my SUV, and leave me the keys to your car. You may need something with four-wheel drive."

Father David looked back at Quinn.

"Everything you need to know is in that envelope. Just do everything it says. Also, there is information in there, explaining where you'll be going."

Quinn shook her head, and leaned in to give him a hug. While hugging her, Father David whispered, "You have the necklace?" Quinn patted her shirt, and nodded her head.

"Can you give my mom a call? Tell her I love her and to stay out of town?"

Father David released Quinn, and said that he would.   Ajax shook his hand.   They loaded everything in the back, and climbed into the big SUV.

Chapter 11

While Ajax pulled out of the driveway, Quinn opened the envelope. Inside was a set of keys, a pre-paid phone, a stack of money, and a few papers. The first paper was a map, the second was written directions, and the third was a note that read:

> *If you are reading this letter, you are already on the road. Everything that you need came with this letter. The map and directions may seem a little over the top, but I don't want you taking shortcuts. In the back hatch, there are two large gas reserves. I don't want you stopping for gas, just in case you're followed. The directions I gave you will make it so no person can follow without stopping for gas. When you get to the town, refill those reserves, just in case.*

You will be going to my father's hunting cabin, just over the state line. Just make sure you don't make any unneeded stops. There is plenty of cash for things needed once you get there. The detective will be making a personal call to a state trooper friend up there, so, you'll have help if you need it. The state trooper's name is Greg Smith. At the cabin, you'll have everything, even a landline. The cabin isn't heated by gas, but there's plenty of wood for the wood stove. There's electricity and running water. If you run into any issues on the road, just use the prepaid phone. I put the numbers you'll need in it.

I want you two to be safe. May God be with you.

P.S.   There are a couple of big thermoses in the back seat.

Father David

"Do you think they'll put an end to this before they find out where we are?" Quinn asked.

Ajax turned his head for a minute, but could only see the profile of her face. She looked sad. He reached over and patted her knee, hoping to give her a little comfort.

"Honestly, I don't know. What I can say is, I won't let anything happen to you. Try and get some sleep, okay?"

Quinn yawned, and nodded her head in agreement. Pulling her pillow from the back seat, she laid it against the window, and fell fast asleep.

Ajax glanced at her again. "Nothing gonna happen to her," he thought to himself.

Two hours into the drive, Ajax reached in the back seat, and grabbed a thermos. He carefully poured some piping hot, black coffee into a mug that was in the cup holder. He blew the steam from the top, and took a few sips. He was starting to get stiff. He glanced at the map. It showed that there was a back road coming up for a pit stop, and to add gas to the car.

"A blessing! After I'm finished with this mug, I'll be hitting a large oak tree."

Quinn gasped lightly in her sleep, distracting Ajax from his last though. He looked over at her, and she was still sound asleep. He worried about her sleeping so much with a concussion, but he knew she was exhausted.

Quinn was sleeping well. She fogged in and out of dreamland. For a moment, she was in the arms of the beautiful angel. He whispered things that she was destined to do. "Save him. God needs him to live." The dream would fade, and then come back. It was more of a memory than a dream.

"My father wouldn't harm me, or someone I know. Would he?" Ajax thought to himself. He knew his father as a stern, strict but easy-going man. His father was hard on him, but he didn't seem the type to hurt his family. His father'd told him that he was only hard on Ajax because he wanted him to be somebody someday.

"Maybe I didn't become the hateful bastard he wanted me to be," Ajax thought, suddenly angered. The anger was getting the better of him. Ajax's jaw was sore from clenching his teeth, and he could feel the vein in his forehead throb.

A few minutes later, Ajax pulled onto a small, narrow dirt road. The moment the car jolted, Quinn shot up in panic.

"Hey, it's okay. Just turning off for our first stop."

Quinn took a deep, shaky breath, and sat back against the seat. Ajax handed her the mug of coffee he'd been drinking out of, and gave her a relaxed smile.

"How long was I out?" Quinn asked, downing the last of the coffee.

"Almost three hours."

Quinn noticed that the sun was already coming up. She ran her fingers through her tangled hair, which was almost standing up on her head. She groaned, and pulled it to the top of her head, into a messy bun.

"Y'know, you have the wildest bed head I've ever seen!" Ajax chuckled.

Quinn went a little red.

"It's gorgeous, though," he added, with a wink.

If she hadn't been noticeably blushing a moment before, she was now.

Ajax knew, but he kept his eyes on the dirt road ahead, and pulled into an even narrower dirt road. Just a mile up the road, they pulled over. It looked like an off the track camping site. There was a fire pit and, about one hundred feet from that, there was an outhouse.

"Looks like we got lucky, sweetheart." Ajax pointed to the small wooden outhouse.

"Looks like I won't be using an oak tree."

Quinn laughed, and refilled the coffee mug.

"You go first," Quinn said, drinking the hot coffee.

While Ajax was in the outhouse, Quinn got some sandwiches, chips, and pops from the cooler, and put them in the front seat.

"Hey, Quinn, hit the pot. We're down to less than ten minutes before we have to get back on the road. I'll restore the gas tank while you do your thing."

Quinn grabbed a bottle of water from the cooler, and headed to the outhouse. She dropped the water right outside the door, and went it. It was quite small, but didn't smell as bad as she'd thought it would. When she was finished, she opened the bottle of water, and washed her hands and face.

She watched as Ajax finished up. He seemed to be lost in thought. He removed the V-neck shirt that he had on. It looked like he might have got gas on it. Quinn walked over, and took his shirt from his hands.

"Would hate for you to go up in flames," she said, with a teasingly smile.

She rinsed the shirt with water from the bottle, and then handed the rest of the bottle to Ajax, so he could rinse his hands. Quinn dabbed a little of her body soap on the shirt, and rubbed it together. She laid it on the back seat to dry.

"Gimme the keys. I put some food up front, and maybe you can get some rest."

Ajax nodded, handed her the keys, and hopped, shirtless, into the passenger seat.

"Distraction while driving, not good," she said to herself, smiling.

"What're you smiling at?" Ajax asked out his window.

Quinn shook her head, and climbed in the other side.

Chapter 12

A little after four in the afternoon, Quinn pulled up to a little gas station/general store. The swaying sign above read: "ADAM & EVE'S." It was no bigger than the average twenty-four-hour go-to market. It was a sight, though, made in the log cabin style, with a long covered porch. Like something that would be seen in an old Western. That was the biggest thing in this town. Across the two-lane road, which looked like it didn't see many cars, was a little building with two doors. One door read, "Post Office," and the one next to it read, "Police."

Quinn pulled up to one of the two gas pumps. She looked over at Ajax, who was still adjusting from being asleep to being awake. He squinted out of his window.

"ADAM & EVE'S."   He looked at me, and raised a brow.

"That's what it says," Quinn chuckled.

Ajax jumped out of the car, still very shirtless, and stretched. Quinn laughed when he made the growling sound as he was stretching.

She reached into the car, and grabbed a black tank-top out of the duffel bag; she tossed it over the car to Ajax, who jumped and caught it.

"I'll fill the tank and top off the reserves," Ajax said passing her a wad of money. "Wanna run in and ask Adam and Eve for some food supplies?"

"Yeah," Quinn said, stifling a yawn.

Quinn slowly opened the front door to the store. The door creaked loudly, and a little funny-sounding bell rang from above. The floors were old hardwood, with spots of missing varnish, and it smelled of pine trees. As she made her way past the counter, there was still no sign of anyone. All along the walls were heads of animals that'd been hunted. Just the wall she was looking at had a large head of a black bear; a few deer heads, most with a large rack; and in the corner was a mounted elk's head.

"Hello! Is anyone here?" Quinn called out.

It was silent for a moment, then she heard a door close in the back.

"Yeah, yeah. So sorry for making ya wait. We don't get too many people comin' yonder till huntin' season," said a voice, making its way toward the store part.

Quinn smiled when she saw a little old man making his way behind the counter. He had short, slicked-back, gray hair, and he was no taller than five foot seven. He was sporting a white tee, topped with overalls. Quinn noticed that he had kind eyes; they were very bright for someone his age. Quinn stepped up to the counter, and gave him a sweet smile.

"No problem, Sir. This is a nice little place ya got here."

"Oh, thank ya, Dear, We love this place, too. What can I fetch?"

"Well, I see no freezers. I'm guessing you don't sell meat?"

The old man chuckled. "Little Lady, we do have, and sell, meat. I don't have too much of chicken and beef stocked, but I do have a bit o' deer, wild boar, and bear in my freezer."

Quinn smiled. "I've never tried bear, so let that be the first thing on the list. Also, give me a little of everything. At least enough for a week worth of camping. Gonna need some eggs, bread, milk, coffee, butter, rice, taters, and veggies. Oh, and some junk food and pop."

The old man jotted fast, as Quinn spoke. He nodded here and there, and made "Uh huh" sounds in between.

"Here ya are, Little Lady. These bags're reusable, so when ya leave town, just drop 'em back off here, or come back for a refill." The little man set the bags down on the counter. "Looks like your total today is thirty eight dollars and fourteen cents."

"Yes, Sir, here ya go," Quinn said, handing over the money. "How much do I owe you for the gas?" .

The man gave her back change, and said, "That was put on Father David's account, and by the way, my name is Adam."

"Well, Adam, it's really nice to meet ya. My name is Quinn."

"I know who ya is. Father Dave speaks about the people of his town quite often."

Quinn smiled, and picked up her bags.

"Thank you so much for everything. I'll see ya around."

The little old man followed Quinn outside, and gave her a wave, once the food was placed inside the vehicle. Quinn waved back, and climbed back into the SUV.

"You'll never guess who that was,", Quinn said, smiling.

Ajax started the car and pulled it onto the road.

"Would I be right if I said that was most likely not Eve?"

Quinn gave his arm a little shove.

"That was Adam. He's a sweetheart."

Ajax rubbed his arm, and made a face, like he was in pain.

"We should be at the cabin in about ten minutes. From what the map looks like, it may be waterfront. Maybe Father David has some fishing gear stored up there."

"Maybe,", Quinn replied, smiling. "That would definitely be fun. Catch some fish, and make 'em for dinner one day."

About ten minutes later, they pulled up to the hunting cabin. It looked better than they both expected. It looked more like a log cabin on a lake.

Ajax walked around to the other side of the car, where Quinn was already standing. Ajax noticed she looked tired, and her face was still quite swollen. The bruising looked a lot worse. She seemed calm, for everything that'd happened. He watched the profile of her face, as she gazed peacefully at the lake. After a few moments, Ajax took her hand, and led her closer to the lake. He really liked the smile she gave him when he put his hand in hers.

They were by the lake for a while before Ajax released her hand; he put a hand on her back, and gave it a light rub.

"Why don't you go in and get some rest? Take a bath and get some sleep. I'll unpack the SUV, and put stuff where it belongs."

Quinn smiled a weary smile, and nodded her head.

"Okay, I'll grab the duffel bag. A bath sounds great right about now."

Chapter 13

Quinn took the key, and unlocked the heavy cabin door. It opened softly, with hardly any noise. She pushed the door back with the toe of her foot, far enough open for her to enter. What she entered looked to be the living and dining area. The living room was large, with a huge, wood-burning fireplace. It was definitely a hunting cabin, for sure. The walls were covered with the heads of the animals someone had caught. The couch, love seat, and chairs were all wood-framed, and the cushions were printed retro-gauche. She'd known people who had these. They had pictures of cabins or animals printed on the cushions. On each side of every chair was an end table that was made from logs, and the coffee table matched.

Quinn took a few steps in, and noticed that the kitchen was just off the dining room. The dining room table was made from logs, as well, but looked like a picnic table, with a chair at the heads of the table. It was big enough to seat twelve people. The place was something out of a magazine. The stove in the kitchen was vintage; it had to be from the 1950s. The stove was over four feet long, and had six burners on the range, and a flat-surfaced grill. The beauty also had double broilers and double ovens. The stove also sported a large warming cabinet and storage rail, which held spices. On the kitchen's back wall, again, was a vintage fridge. Quinn was blown away at the beauty of it all.

Quinn made her way down the long hall. There was a room to the right, which homed a queen-sized bed, two dressers, and a window that took up the wall from floor to ceiling. Across the hall was a small bathroom. A few feet down from that was a bedroom that looked just like the last. The door at the end of the hall was closed. She pushed it open with the palm of her hand. The room was just a tad bit bigger than the other two rooms. It had two full-size beds, two sets of bunk beds, and built-in storage. There was a sliding door, which led out to a deck at the far end of the room. Again, everything was wooden, and downright gorgeous.

Quinn went to pull open what she thought was the closet, and found the second bath. The bath tub was a cast-iron claw-foot, and very deep. She shut the door, dropped the bag to the floor, and undressed. While the tub filled, she took some over-the-counter pain meds, and drank from the sink. As, soon as her body sank to the bottom of the tub, her bone ceased aching.

Quinn forced herself out when the waters turned cold, and dressed. Sleep was taking over, and the meds were working. She had but a mild ache from her face and ribs. After she tossed on a long night shirt and shorts, she walked into the bedroom, and crawled in the nearest full-size bed. She quickly drifted fast asleep.

After Ajax did some exploring of the grounds, he unpacked the SUV, and put all the food away. He was blown away at how nice this hunting cabin was. He thought he was going to be walking into four walls, dirt floors, and a wood stove. Boy was he wrong!

"Father David has some nice digs," he thought to himself, as he walked around, locking up. Ajax found the first small bath, and cleaned himself up. He was hungry, but more tired than anything. He went looking to find where Quinn had gone off too. The first two bedrooms were empty. He noticed the door at the end of the hall was open. There was where he found Quinn, passed out on top of the quilt. She was curled up on her side, and her hair was still wet. He walked over, and covered her with a fluffy, brown blanket, which was neatly folder at the end of her bed. She didn't budge. He smiled to himself.

"She's out," he thought.

Ajax kicked off everything but his boxers, climbed into the empty full-size bed, and covered himself with the sheet and blanket that were there. The bed was so soft, it was devouring him whole. He lay still. It didn't take long for him to drift off to sleep.

Chapter 14

Quinn knew she was dreaming, when she woke up lying next to a doe and a fawn, sleeping peacefully. The greenest grass and the prettiest lilies surrounded her. The air smelled of cotton candy and vanilla beans. The scent was warm and welcoming. This time, she was in a clearing, which was surrounded by the largest trees she'd ever seen. This time, the sky looked like the normal sky on earth, except that the sun was much larger, and gave off warmth when the cool breeze wafted through. Quinn was still amazed at how delightful this place really was. The smell of cotton candy became stronger, and she smiled to herself.

"Hi, Michael," she said aloud, knowing he was standing right behind her.

"Hi, My Child," he responded.

Michael came around, and sat down in front of her. His eyes were a brown she'd never seen before. They were soothing. He smiled at her.

"I take it everything has come back to you?"

"Yes, Michael, I know what I must do," she said, plucking a blade of grass near her bare feet.

"You do know it's a choice? Free will, and all."

Quinn looked up at him.

"I couldn't choose the alternative, even with free will, Michael. How could I watch something happen and not do anything to prevent it? I know this could go a few different ways. I hope for the good ending, but I'm ready for the worst, if it happens."

Michael leaned over, and kissed her forehead, as a parent does to a child.

"You are just like your dad...."

Before, Quinn could respond, she was painfully jerked out of her dream existence.

After what felt like ten minutes of being stretched and tortured, she landed on a hard, jagged, and ashy surface. She rolled onto her stomach, in a coughing fit that made her ribs throb more than they already had been. Pain shot through her body again, as she vomited from the aggressiveness of the pain. When her stomach was empty, and there was nothing left to discard, she rolled back over to her back. Her body trembled from the pain. She was in a daze, and felt like she was moving. She grunted, as her body was dragged over sharp pebbles. She lifted her head enough to see what was going on. It was something horrible-looking. It walked on two legs. What skin it did have was hanging slightly off its body, like it'd been burned. Not once did it turn to face its victim. Even though she was being dragged painfully, she couldn't fight. She felt as if she was frozen, and couldn't even use her voice to scream.

Quinn's eyes flew open, and she screamed out in agony. Her skin felt like it was being burned to the bone.

"You stupid, stupid girl! You could have avoided all of this!"

Dantanian stood looking down at Quinn. His eyes were angry, and very scary-looking. He grabbed her thigh with a hand that was red as flames. Quinn screamed out again, in pain. It made her body shudder and shake. Dantanian stood back up and paced.

"Are you ready to let things take the course that was meant to be?"

Quinn couldn't speak. She still felt as if she was on fine.

After a few minutes, Dantanian waved his hands, and all the pain disappeared.

"Answer me now, Girl!" he screamed.

Quinn didn't want to answer the demon. She knew more pain would come to follow.

"No," she simply replied.

Dantanian drew out from his palm what looked like a whip, cased in lava.

Quinn panicked, and reached for the cross around her neck. It was not there. With a snap of his fingers, her arms flew above her head, and all her limbs were pressed down hard to the ground. She knew what type of pain was coming, and there was nothing she could do about it. She tensed up, and waited for the worse to come. When the first strike came, she screamed out in pain, and Dantanian smiled sweetly, enjoying the pain he was causing.

Chapter 15

Ajax flew from the bed when he heard a loud thump and a skin-curling scream. It took him a moment for his eyes to adjust to the darkness of the bedroom. When he could see, he saw Quinn, flat on her back on the floor. To him, it looked like she was seizing. When he crouched beside her, she let out another scream. Tears were streaming down her face. He looked down, and noticed a red, swollen welt on her leg.

"What the hell is going on?" he yelled. "Quinn, wake up! Wake up now!" he yelled, patting her hand.

"Dammit!" he growled, frustrated.

Right before she let out another scream, he watched as her nightshirt ripped across the torso, and her bare skin singed.

Ajax ran to the bathroom, and turned on the cold water in the tub. He returned to Quinn's side. He reached out and untangled the flat sheet from her bed, and placed it over her. She let out another scream, and a bloody welt came across her shoulder and chest. Ajax carefully lifted her in his arms, and carried her into the bathroom. One foot at a time, he climbed in. His breath caught from the icy cold water. Slowly, he lowered them both into the tub. The cold had him cringing, but didn't seem to faze Quinn just yet. She was still shaking with pain, as another scorching welt showed up on her neck and upper arm. Ajax shook her a tad bit. Her not responding to the pain, or the cold water, was more terrifying than her screaming.

"Dammit, Quinn, wake the hell up!"

Ajax turned to his side, and let her fall all the way into the icy water. That seemed to do the trick. Ajax saw her eyes fly open. He grabbed her out of the water, and slipped back into the sitting position. He pulled her over him, so her upper body was no longer in the water.

Quinn was face-first against his chest. She was trembling and whimpering. Ajax held her tight, brushing her hair off her face.

"I gotcha. I gotcha. It's alright; you're alright. It's over now," Ajax repeated over and over, trying to soothe her. Ajax used his foot to turn on the hot water, till the tub heated up to a temperature hot enough to warm them up.

After a while, Quinn was still holding on to him tightly, and her trembling had slowed down. Ajax could feel the warm tears on his chest. All he could do was gently rub her back, and keep whispering words of comfort. He wasn't sure whether he was comforting her at all, but that wasn't going to stop him from trying. After what he'd seen happening, he needed those words of comfort, as well. His heart was thumping from the stuff he'd experienced this very night.

When the water started cooling again, Ajax tried to get up. Quinn didn't let go.

"Okay, I gotcha," he said, carefully standing up. Her arms were locked around his shoulders, and her legs swung over his arm. It took forever, but when he finally got them out of the tub, he took her over to her bed, and grabbed the blankets. He grabbed more off the bed he was sleeping on. They were still soaked, but there was no way he could convince her to let go to get changed. So, he took all the blankets to the living room, sat down in front of the fireplace, and started a fire. He wrapped them up in all the bedding he'd brought out.

After an hour, Ajax felt Quinn's body fully relax. She seemed to have cried herself to sleep. The tears on his chest were proof. Ajax was still in shock over everything that'd happened. He'd never seen anything like it in his life. He thought back to the day he went to visit her.

She was in the shower, so he sat on her bed to wait. The nightshirt was singed, just like the one she was wearing now. He shook his head, kicking himself for not believing her then.

Ajax laid them both down next to the fireplace. She was still stuck to him, as she'd been since she woke up. Even asleep, she did not let go. Ajax stayed awake as long as he could. His eyes grew so heavy that he couldn't stop sleep from invading him.

Quinn woke up with her face snuggled up into Ajax's neck. Her muscles ached from how tightly she was holding on to him all through the night. She relaxed her body, but still felt she wasn't ready to let go. She felt safe, for the time being. After last night, her choice didn't seem as clear as it had before.

"I'm not gonna let him win," she thought to herself. "I can't let him win."

The fear of sleep crept in. "If he can take over my dreams, sleep will be something of the past."

"How long have you been awake?" Ajax's rough morning voice broke through her thoughts.

"Not too long," Quinn whispered from the crook of his neck.

"You alright?"

Quinn nodded.

Ajax gave her a squeeze, and lightly kissed the top of her head.

Quinn smiled to herself.

"As much as I enjoy you this close, I think it best if we get off this floor. I also really have to use the bathroom," he said, with a deep, raspy chuckle.

Quinn nodded again, and slowly unwrapped herself from Ajax.

When she was in a sitting position, Ajax knelt right in front of her.

"Hey," he said, softly. "Are you sure you're okay?"

Quinn gave him a small smile, and said, "Thank you."

Ajax stood up, and pulled her with him.

"I would totally kiss you right now, if I didn't have morning breath," Ajax said, with a handsome wink.

Quinn watched after him with a slight grin, as he bolted for the small bath. She stood up, and folded all the bedding, placing it neatly on the chair.

Quinn went into the other bathroom, but left the bathroom door cracked, still a little scared to be completely alone. She stepped into the shower, and let the hot water pelt on her skin. The welts were still there, but not as dark, and they were pretty much closed. They still hurt, though, along with her other injuries. Quinn took her time, and washed her hair and body before shutting off the shower. She pulled in the large, fluffy towel to dry off, and got dressed.

When she walked out of the bathroom, Ajax was sitting on the freshly made bed.

"Something told me you wouldn't want to be alone," Ajax said, standing up to close the gap between them.

"I left some lunch, pop, and your pills on the dresser."

Ajax stepped in a little closer, and lowered his head. He was close enough that she could feel the heat from his mouth. Ajax reached down, and twined their hands together. Quinn looked down at her hand in his.

"Hey, how are you feeling?"

Quinn looked back up at Ajax. "Better now," she replied, with a small smile.

Ajax stood there for a long moment. He wasn't sure he wanted to let go. He was sure of how he was feeling at this moment, and he knew he needed to get it out of his head right now.

"I'm gonna go get a quick shower, while you eat."

As hard as it was, he removed his hand from hers. He allowed himself to sneak a kiss on her temple, which left her blushing. Ajax enjoyed making her blush.

In the shower, Ajax drowned himself in the memories of the early morning. Just remembering it made his gut roll and his chest tighten.

"Jeeze, I thought it was only my father we needed to be worried about." he thought to himself. "This is so much worse than my father."

Ajax's hands started shaking. "No. This isn't gonna scare me," he repeated to himself, over and over again.

When Ajax came out of the bathroom, Quinn was going through the built-in cabinets. She had on a pair of yoga pants and a white tank top. Her locks were falling down her back, and almost reached her rear end.

She turned around, put her hands on her hips and smiled. "What are you looking at?"

All Ajax could think was, even with the busted lip and bruised face, she was still very cute.

When Ajax didn't respond, she put her face in the cabinet again, and came back out with a couple boxes.

"Look what I found! Wanna pretend it's raining, make some coffee and play some old board games? Look, here's Candy Land, and Chutes and Ladders!"

Ajax laughed. "How can I say no? I'll go start the coffee; you get this mess set up."

About twenty minutes later, they were cross-legged on the living room floor with their coffee. So far, Ajax was the winner of all the games. He was sure to brag about it, as well. They ate dinner while playing cards. The day had turned to night, and they lit the fireplace, put up the games, and made some hot cocoa.

Quinn was still not ready for bed. She dreaded falling asleep, so she put on the movie, *Jaws*, and they sat and watched it. Quinn enjoyed sitting

right next to Ajax. He felt safe. Well, at least till
she had to close her eyes.

Chapter 17

Quinn lay in her bed, staring up at the ceiling. She'd been there for a couple hours now. The room was dark, but the moon shining in made things easier to make out. When the tree outside shifted in the breeze, it made beautiful art shadows on the wall. If she stared at it too long, she started feeling her eyes drift. On the other bed, she could hear Ajax breathing softly. He lay awake for a while, as well; Quinn thought he was fearful of falling asleep, too. Quinn acted as if she was asleep, so he would relax. Her face and ribs were throbbing and sore, but she didn't want to take anything, because the pain helped her stay awake.

Quinn woke up in a panic; she realized she'd drifted to sleep. She turned and looked at the bedside clock; it was four in the morning. She quietly slipped out of bed in her long t-shirt, and walked barefoot to the kitchen, where she made a pot of coffee, and set some sausage and bacon out to defrost. Then she added wood to the fireplace.

When the coffee finished brewing, she poured herself a mug, and sat right in front of the fireplace. She wished she could contact her mom. Maybe she could go to town later, and give her a call. She was told no cell phones, and the cabin was for emergencies only. To kill the time till the sun came up, she opened a hunting magazine. She was flabbergasted at all the things she learned. There was an article about why hunting season falls at a certain time of the year, and why some can be hunted more often. She learned the differences between various type of bows and fishing rods. On the last page, there was a picture of a bearded man, kneeling down, holding the head of a large deer, with huge antlers. She was amazed that the man sat out there ten hours before he shot that deer.

"What the heck do they do out there that whole time?" she wondered.

She couldn't imagine sitting for ten hours with nothing to do but wait.

"I guess my mom was right. When you're patient, good things will come," she thought .

When she looked up from the magazine, the sun was coming up. She put the magazine back, and went to the kitchen. In a casserole dish, she combined chopped bacon, sausage, eggs, onion, green peppers, and spinach; she popped it in the oven. She knew it would take a while to cook, so she refilled her mug, and decided to get some fresh air. She walked around the porch to the back of the cabin. The birds were chirping, and the wind was light, but heaven-sent. She could smell the pine trees and the musky smell from the lake when the wind blew. She put her mug on the railing, and stretched. She didn't feel sleepy at the moment. She grabbed her mug, and went back to the trail that led to the lake. Quinn could hear the stones crunch into the earth as she walked. The ground was cool under her bare feet. When she reached the dock, she sat cross-legged at the very end. The water was rippling toward her, and the lapping sounds of the water relaxed her body. She sat there, sipping her coffee and talking to God: a conversation for just the two of them. It was something she hadn't done since she left home. She touched her chest, where the crucifix lay. She smiled to herself, because it made her feel safe.

The sound of footsteps brought her out of her prayer. She turned to see Ajax making his way with a basket.

"Breakfast beach-side?" he said, when he was only a few feet away.

Quinn swiveled her body toward him.

"Yes. I was about to come in and take it out. I guess I lost track of time. Easy to do out here."

Ajax smiled. "I can see that."

He sat down and unpacked the casserole, coffee, and dishes.

"How did you sleep?" Ajax asked.

"I slept okay," she replied.

They sat in silence, and ate. Ajax enjoyed breakfast, or he was just really hungry, because he ate over half of it.

"Mmm, that was good! Thank you," Ajax said, sipping his coffee.

"Well, thank you for the compliment, and you're welcome," Quinn replied.

"So, what've you been up to out here?" Ajax asked.

"Enjoying the sights." Quinn said simply, then added, "Do you think we could go to town today? I'd really like to call my mom, or even send her an e-mail."

Ajax finished packing up the basket, and smiled.

"Sure, I don't see why not. Wanna head back, put away the food, and get dressed, then we can head to town?"

The ride to town was unbearable for Quinn. The movement of the car made her extremely tired. Her eyes kept closing, but the fear and panic were mighty enough to pry them open again. For distraction, she glanced aside at Ajax, who was concentrating on avoiding the huge, car-swallowing potholes on the long, dirt road. The afternoon sun shone brightly, and made him squint his eyes.

"Another silly thing that he makes look good. How does he do that? I look constipated when I squint," Quinn thought, trying hard not to laugh at herself.

"You checkin' me out again?" Ajax asked, sneaking a peek in her direction.

Quinn could feel the heat rising to her cheeks.

"Maybe."

Quinn bit her lip, holding back a laugh. Her confession made his face do all kinds of funny things.

"Uh huh, I see what you're up to. Tryin' to play at my games." Ajax said, raising a brow, and blowing out an evil chuckle.

They chit-chatted the rest of the way to town, until they got to Adam and Eve's.

Ajax stood under the sign rubbing his chin and cheek.

"I still can't get over the fact that Adam and Eve found each other," Ajax said, shaking his head.

Quinn just smiled at him, and walked into the store. There was no sign of human life.

"Adam!" Quinn called. "Adam, it's Quinn!"

She heard a thump from the back, and started walking in that direction.

"Adam, are you alright?"

"Yeah. Yeah, I'm alright. I'll be right there."

After a moment, she saw Adam making his way toward the front of the store.

"Sorry, little lady. I think them boxes back there're getting' bigger than me," Adam said, smiling.

"Well, can I give you a hand?" Quinn asked sweetly.

Ajax walked up behind Quinn, shook Adam's hand, and said, "I'll give you a hand, Sir. Just tell me where you need me."

Adam smiled in appreciation. "Why, thank you, young man. Sometimes, I wish I were still young."

Adam paused for a minute. It looked like he was remembering his younger years. His eyes sparkled..

"Just go right through the back, and to the right. You'll see the mess of boxes I was trying to load on the shelf."

Ajax patted Quinn's back, and took the directions Adam gave.

"What y'all come in ta down today for?" Adam asked, rubbing his hands together.

"Well, I was wondering how I can contact my mom. Can I send an e-mail, or call?"

Adam sighed, and looked a little saddened.

"I'm sorry, honey. We ain't got no internet, and Father David said no phone use."

Adam walked around the counter, and handed Quinn a pad of paper and a marker.

"I'll tell you what, though. I'm gonna be running up to Bolden Falls this afternoon. If you write out a message, I'll call Father David, and have him call ya mamas."

"Oh, thank you so much, Adam," she replied, and gave him a hug.

"Darlin', you are welcome."

After Quinn and Ajax wrote their letters, they gave them to Adam.

"Ajax, would you mind taking the ride with me?" Adam asked. "It's a fast trip. Just giving Father David a call, and dropping off some money at the bank."

Ajax looked at Quinn, and then back at Adam.

"Will Quinn be safe here?" Ajax asked

"She sure will. Sheriff's right 'cross yonder. I really don't like to leave Eve alone."

This was the first time Quinn heard Adam speak of Eve.

"She has some old-timers, I like to call it. It ain't bad yet, but she's depressed because of it. We were told a few weeks ago. Now, she doesn't talk much, and she won't leave the house. She's a stubborn mama."

Quinn agreed to stay back with Eve.

"There's plenty of food in the fridge for lunch. I'm locking up till me and Ajax get back," Adam told her.

Quinn watched as they pulled out of the lot, and drove off. Across the street, she saw the cruiser sitting there. Not a soul around. The slight breeze rattled the little bushes and trees that were around the building across the street.

"It's a ghost town," she whispered to herself.

Chapter 18

Quinn found her way to Adam and Eve's home. The door was already open, so she just walked in. It wasn't large at all. From where she stood, at the door, she could see the kitchen, with a little table and chairs, and the living room. To the right, a door was open, exposing a bathroom. To the left was a closed door she expected was their bedroom. It was small, but very comfortable and warm. A smell set her mouth watering, and her tummy grumbling. Their home smelled of fresh coffee and apple pie. She noticed that there was an apple pie sitting on the stove.

Opening the fridge, she saw a pot of beef stew, and sliced up, homemade bread. While Quinn warmed up the food on the stove, she hummed her favorite Christian song. When everything was warming up, she found two plates, and set them on the table, along with two tall glasses of ice-cold milk. She folded some napkins, laid the forks on them, and put the spoons knives on the other side of the plates. She'd just finished with the table, when the bedroom door opened.

Eve stood in the half-opened doorway. She was quite a beautiful woman. She had long, white hair, pulled into a bun. Her face looked soft around her big, blue eyes. Her face was wrinkled with age. She was of average height, but a little on the thin side. She wore nice dress pants with a flower-printed blouse. The only thing that didn't go with her outfit was the pair of bulky bunny slippers that covered her feet.

"Good afternoon, Mrs. Eve. Are ya hungry?"

"It's just Eve," was her only response.

Eve walked over, and sat down. Quinn sat across from her, and smiled warmly. Then she bowed her head to pray.

"Lord, we are truly thankful for the food to nourish our bodies. I pray for the safety and health of my new friends. Please watch over us, especially in our trying times. Lord, can I ask for a personal and selfish request? Please look after my mama, Mrs. Eve, and all great women like them. Amen"

"Amen," Eve echoed.

They ate lunch in complete silence. Quinn was a little uncomfortable. She didn't know Eve will enough to know what she was thinking. Eve looked up at Quinn from time to time. No expression whatsoever was on her face. When they'd finished their meal, Quinn washed up the dishes, and put away the leftovers. She hummed as she worked. Eve still sat in the chair, watching her.

"I loved that song you were humming," Eve said

Quinn had already put the pie and coffee on the table.

"I love church music, it lifts my spirits," Quinn replied. Again sitting across from Eve, Quinn noticed Eve had already poured the coffee, and sliced and served the pie. Quinn took the first bite of pie, and washed it down with coffee.

"Mmm, did you make this?" Quinn asked, amazed by the flavor.

"I sure did. The pie made it out of the oven before the sun came up," Eve answered.

"I do have to say, quite honestly, this is the best pie I have ever had!" Quinn said, scooping in another spoonful.

Eve's eye suddenly brightened, and a perfect smile dawned upon her face. This expression made her look so alive.

"Thank you, my dear."

Quinn and Eve went on for another hour or two. Neither of them moved from the table. They talked about their favorite Bible verses and favorite Christian music. Eve told her about her younger years, and how she met Adam. She admitted to the name thing shocking them, as well.

"We guess it was meant to be. Two God-loving people meeting under the names of the first humans created, don't ya think?"

Quinn slapped her thigh in laughter.

"My friend, Ajax, said the same thing. Well, in other words."

They were both laughing when Adam walked into the room.

Quinn noticed a confused look on his face, but it soon turned into a bright grin. It was nice to see his wife happy and smiling again.

"What's ya ladies cackling about?" Adam asked, walking up behind Eve and pecking her cheek with his lips. Eve's smile faltered, and she looked at her husband.

"I feel so alive," she told him, with glistening eyes. "I'm sorry about the last few months," she added.

Adam didn't respond. He just smiled and kissed her: a long, sweet kiss.

"God is good, my dear," he whispered back.

They smiled at each other for a long while before noticing they had an audience. Eve looked at Quinn, and then back at her husband.

"Where did you find this angel?" she asked him.

"They landed here, darlin'. I'll fill you in later," he said, winking at her.

"This is Ajax," Adam told Eve.

Ajax came in, and gave Eve a peck on the cheek.

"Good evening, Eve. You're prettier than your husband described."

Eve looked Ajax over, as any grandmother would.

"Quinn, you didn't mention your friend being handsome and sweeter than my apple pie."

Quinn blushed.

"I think she gets flustered by my good looks," Ajax said winking at Quinn.

The whole room roared with the heavenly sound of laughter.

After everyone settled down, Quinn warmed up some bread and stew for the guys, and then sat on the back porch with Eve. The evening air was warm, with a cool breeze. The whole day had passed, and evening was drawing to an end. The sun was low on the horizon, but the sky was so clear, and dimly lit. The porch light gave off a soft glow, and the crickets began to speak to one another.

"It's so lovely here," Quinn said to no one particular.

"I moved here 38 years ago, and I still think so, too," Eve said.

"How long have you been married?"

"Almost 45 years. I married when I was 22 and Adam was 25."

Quinn smiled. Eve had a proud look on her face.

"Any children?"

Eve's eyes brightened.

"None of our own, but we fostered kids in their late teens, so they would have a place to call home when they aged out of the system. We fostered 20 teens, and 13 of them still call and visit, and we meet for dinner every Christmas."

"What happened to the others?" Quinn asked curiously.

"They had it rough in the system. We got to them too late. I did what I could, but they were too far gone. A few of them went on to the good Lord, and the other, well, I dunno. I do have to say that each and every one of them blessed me."

Quinn took all that in, and let it sit there a while.

"I hope, someday, to have what you have, Eve."

"Someday, you will, my child. Someday, you will. The Lord knows what he's doing."

Chapter 19

On the road to the cabin, Ajax concentrated on the road. Being dark and all, he didn't want to hit a deer. He was lost in thoughts of the day he'd just had. He was surrounded by nice people who didn't want squat from him. Ajax thought of the trip to Bolden Falls with Adam.

"He had me laughing most of the trip," he thought.

The ride was maybe 45 minutes northeast from where they were. Bolden Falls was another small town. Not too small, though. It had more than three buildings, and a higher population.

"Looked kinda like an old Western town," he thought.

They were only there for about 45 minutes. It was just enough time for Adam to do what he needed, and to pass the messages from Quinn and Ajax.

On the way back, Adam told Ajax about his wife falling into depression, and how he missed her so, and how the last few months had been so lonely.

After getting back, and entering the store, Adam looked at Ajax, and raised his eyebrows.

"Are they laughing?"

"Seems so," Ajax responded.

The look on Adam's face when he entered the small apartment was like seeing his best friend after being apart for years. The way he held her and kissed her made Ajax believe there were still compassionate people out there. He just hadn't met too many people like this, except this nice couple and Quinn.

"Quinn: I like her a lot. She could be with me. She could make me whole again. It's not that far-fetched, right?" he thought, smiling.

"I know she likes me; I can tell by the way she looks at me. She's just very shy, is all; this is something we shall work on," he thought.

Ajax smiled to himself, thinking about his newest memory. He looked over at Quinn, who'd fallen asleep, beside him in the car. She looked so peaceful. She hadn't looked like this since the night before last.

"That dream took its toll on her, and she's having a hard time shaking it."

He knew, although she was smiling and happy; he knew, under the smile was fear.

"She hasn't really talked about it, and I'm scared to bring it up."

Ajax thought back to that night. His gut turned, remembering the events that took place.

Watching the welts appear still shook him to his core. If someone told him this was possible a few months ago, he would have thought they were crazy. Ajax glanced at Quinn again. The swelling on her face had gone down, her lip had scabbed over, and the welts seemed to completely disappear. He'd seen her clutch her side, so he knew her ribs still hurt, but she never complained.

When Ajax hit the dirt road to the cabin, Quinn sat straight up from a dead sleep.

"Quinn, it's alright; we're almost to the cabin," Ajax said, with a soothing voice, while rubbing her trembling shoulder.

Quinn seemed to be confused and jerky.

"You alright?" Ajax asked, as he pulled up close to the cabin's door, and turned off the SUV. Quinn's eyes were still a little wide.

"Yeah, I think so," she said, avoiding eye contact.

"Are you su…"

"Ajax, I said I was fine," Quinn said, cutting him short, and quickly exiting the SUV.

Stunned, Ajax watched her enter the cabin.

"What the hell was that?" he said to himself out loud.

This was a side that he didn't know she had.

Quinn walked into the cabin, shutting the door behind her. She walked over to the coffee pot, and was about to pour the grounds into the filter. Instead, she walked to the fridge, and took out a Coke, opened it, and walked back over to where she'd left the coffee grounds. She took a drink of the Coke, and shoved a spoonful of coffee grounds in her mouth; she washed it down with some more Coke. The sand's texture made her gut twist, and it took effort to keep it down. She put the spoon in the sink with shaky hands, and finished the whole can of Coke. She rinsed out the can, and put it upside down in the sink.

After the shock wore off, Ajax walked into the cabin. Quinn stood with her back to him. Her hands were gripping the sink, and her head was hung low. Ajax slowly walked up, and placed a hand on her shoulder. When he felt her body relax, he turned her around, and pulled her into a tight hug.

"I'm so sorry I talked to you the way I did."

Ajax felt his shirt tighten on his body, as she balled his clothing into her fist. He could feel how upset she was. He knew her snapping was nothing like her.

"Shh, it's okay. It's alright," Ajax whispered to the top of her head.

"Quinn, is there anything I can do?"

Quinn shook her head against his chest, and pulled her head back a little.

"No. I don't know what got into me; there isn't anything bothering me. I just really don't know where that came from."

Ajax looked down at her. Her eyes told him she was lying to him, and he bet that she didn't even know she was.

"Okay, how about we get some sleep? It's been a long day."

Quinn nodded. "Okay, I'll be there in a sec."

After Ajax left the room, Quinn gagged down a few more spoonfuls of coffee grounds, and washed them down with water from the tap.

When Ajax walked out of the bathroom, Quinn had already changed into her night shirt. She gave him a small smile, as she passed him to go brush her teeth.

She didn't even shut the door. She walked over to the mirror, and slowly brushed her teeth. She took her time, hoping Ajax would fall asleep. After she brushed her teeth, she washed her face, and put on some cream. She felt the caffeine catching up with her. Quinn started to feel restless, and her heart fluttered a little faster. When she couldn't stall any longer, she walked out of the bathroom, and shut off the light.

Ajax was half under his quilt, lying on his back. He was sound asleep. Quinn felt such relief.

Quinn tip-toed to the kitchen, and put on a pot of strong coffee. While the coffee was brewing, she walked over to a bookcase, which held a few notebooks. She found one that was new, and took it back to the kitchen with her. She sat at the dining room table, with coffee, notebook and her thoughts. She wrote a couple letters, and just did a lot of writing about what was coming into her mind at the moment; with the caffeine jitters, her hand moved at lightning speed. She wrote for a long while, until she was starting to get fuzzy from being tired. She came down hard from her caffeine high. She looked at the clock on the wall. It was only four in the morning.

Around four in the morning, Quinn finally came down from her coffee high. Her head started hurting, and her hands became shaky.

"Nope, not happening!" she said to no one.

Quinn walked to the sink, and poured another cup of coffee to chase another couple of spoonfuls of coffee grounds down. Until the coffee started taking effect, she ran in place in the living room, and did some crazy, wild exercises. She didn't normally work out, so she'd no clue what she was doing. When she was winded, and starting to feel a rush of energy, she sat back down, and wrote some more. She only got up to make another pot of coffee, around eight in the morning.

While waiting for the brew, she hid the notebook where she'd found it.

Chapter 20

Ajax slowly woke up to the smell of breakfast and coffee. Half awake, he rolled out of bed, and looked at the clock. It was almost ten in the morning. He pulled on his pants from the day before, and slowly made his way to the kitchen. The smell was amazing.

"What's that smell?" he said, yawning and stretching his arms over his head.

Quinn turned from the coffee maker, and almost dropped the mugs. Ajax was shirtless, with his pants low and undone. Quinn wasn't expecting him to walk out like that.

"Um. Venison steak and eggs," Quinn almost stuttered.

Ajax cocked his head. Quinn ignored his expression, handed him his coffee cup, and walked to the table, where breakfast was waiting.

Ajax noticed Quinn looked tired. She ate slowly; not once did she move her eyes from her plate.

"How'd ya sleep last night?" Ajax asked.

"Okay, I guess. How about you?" Quinn responded, still looking at her food.

"I slept well. Would you like to go on a nature walk after breakfast?"

Quinn stood up, and took their plates to the sink.

"Yeah, I think that would be cool."

Ajax watched as Quinn walked down the hall. "She doesn't look like she's been sleeping at all. Guess I'll have to find out why," He thought.

After about a half hour, Quinn came down the hall, wearing a pair of jeans shorts that were short, but not too short, and a tank top, tucked in. She also sported black walking shoes.

"It seems warmer than norm out there this morning," Quinn said. She could feel his eyes on her.

"Good. Great day for a walk," Ajax said. "I'll go get dressed," Ajax added, as he started down the hall.

Ajax stopped, and tip-toed back; he peeked into the kitchen. Quinn was eating coffee grounds, and washing them down with coffee.

"She's keeping herself awake," he realized.

Later, Ajax met Quinn on the front porch. He'd just tossed on jeans and a white pocket tee. He had a backpack over his shoulder.

"Ready?" he asked.

Quinn nodded, and they walked side by side, until the path started getting narrow. Then, she let Ajax take the lead. The birds sang, and the woods were filled with so much color. She could have been in a watercolor painting, like the ones she'd seen on office walls. They walked for about an hour and a half, until they came upon a small pond, which was connected to the smallest waterfall ever. Quinn walked over, and touched it. The water was a dull color, but everything around it beamed with color and life.

"Oh, my goodness. Come feel this; it's warm!"

Ajax walked up, knelt down, and ran his hands in the water.

"I know. I saw a map at Adam's store."

Quinn frowned a little.

"I wish I'd bought a swimsuit."

Ajax dropped his backpack to the ground. He unzipped it, and dug around for a minute.

"Here, wear these," he said, tossing her a pair of boxers and one of her own sports bras.

She narrowed her eyes.

"I don't wear two piece suits."

Ajax pulled his stuff out, and went behind a tree.

"Didn't have too many choices. I didn't take you as someone who has body issues," Ajax said while dressing.

"I don't. Not perfect, but wasn't gave a lot to work with," she responded too lightly, but not loud enough for Ajax to hear it all.

Quinn dressed behind another tree.   The boxers fit. That was a plus.

She walked out from behind the tree, and hung her clothing on the front branch.

"Come on in!" Ajax yelled.

Quinn walked to the water, and carefully stepped in. The water wasn't as warm as her bath water, but it felt great. Her body relaxed as she got deeper. The ripples of the water lapped at her skin, melting her tension. Soon, she was deep enough to go under. She came up with her eyes closed. When she opened them, Ajax wasn't but two inches from her nose. He was smiling, and his eyes were soft. Quinn was stuck for a minute, looking back. She smiled back at him, and then shoved his head under the water.

Ajax could hear her thrilled laugh from under the water. He came up behind her, and grabbed her sides. Quinn shrieked. Ajax lifted her, and tossed her into the water. She came up, and was laughing.

A little while later, Ajax sat on the bank, watching her do laps.

"She does look good in my shorts," he said, laughing to himself. "Maybe this will wear her out."

Ajax took out some snacks and drinks. He opened a pill bottle, which he'd taken from her medicine cabinet. It was an all-natural sleep aid. He took out the correct dosage, broke it open, and put half of it in her juice drink.

"This should help her sleep."

Ajax found a shortcut home. On the trail back home, Quinn started to slow down. The shortcut only too them 45 minutes.

When they reached the cabin Ajax playfully tossed her over his shoulders, caveman-style, and carried her down the hall. He pretended to body slam her onto the bed he called his. Quinn was already shrieking. Ajax made growling noises, as he tickled her side. Quinn laughed, and yelled at him. Ajax stopped and flopped on his back.

Quinn settled down a bit.

"Hey, I can make us some dinner."

Ajax knew she was looking at getting out of going to sleep, but he could tell she wouldn't make it long.

"Would you just chill with me for a minute? I promise just laying here."

Quinn thought for a minute. She watched as Ajax flop his arm on the pillow behind her, and winked.

"You know you wanna lay with me," he teased.

Quinn nodded and lay down on his arm, trying to hide her red cheek. She turned into his side, and completely relaxed. Ajax used his free arm to pull the covers over them.

Quinn snuggled into his side. "He smells so good," she thought.

"What're you thinking?" she asked.

Quinn could feel the vibration of his deep voice as he spoke.

"I'm thinking that, when this is over, I'm gonna take you on a real date."

A single unnoticed tear escaped her eye.

"I'd like that," she whispered.

Ajax rubbed her upper back. After a few moments, he could feel her body relax, and her breathing changed. It was low and steady. He used his other hand to move the hair from her face. She was peacefully asleep. He lay there for a couple of hours, just looking at her. He wanted to make sure she wasn't going to have that bad dream again. When it seemed everything was safe, he laid his head against hers, and slowly fell asleep.

A clap of thunder startled Ajax awake. The lightning and the thunder made the world outside the windows look like a war zone. The trees were swaying, and he could feel the ground vibrating from where he lay on the bed. He could hear the crackling of branches in the distance, along with the howling of the wind.

"Wow, where did this crap come from?" he thought.

Hey raised his head, and looked down at Quinn, still sleeping. She needed this rest. He noticed she'd fallen asleep in that huge necklace that Father David gave her. She normally put it under her pillow, or on the night stand, before falling asleep. He wasn't sure what it was, but she seemed to always have it.

BANG!

Ajax sat up fast. He knew he heard the front door fly open.

"The wind must be strong," he thought. He looked down at Quinn, who was still out. He got out of bed, and replaced the covers over her.

He walked down the hall, and over to the door. When he reached the doorway, Ajax felt a strong, forceful wind hit his chest, and it sent him flying across the room. He hit the wall, crashing into a glass memory keeper. He hit the wall so hard that he thought he was going to pass out. His eyes couldn't focus for the longest time. He tried to stand up, but his legs didn't cooperate. His eyesight started to focus; his ears started ringing. Ajax grunted in pain, getting up on his knees.

When his senses and pain settled a little, he looked up at the doorway, and there stood a tall, dark figure, with a long dress coat blowing in the wind.

Chapter 21

He stood there in the darkness of night. He didn't move. He reeked of confidence and hatred. When the lighting flashed, Ajax could see the man's features. His eyes were as black as coal, and the long, black hair, pulled back from his face, matched them. He seemed to be just a hair taller than Ajax, with a thin, but fit, build. Ajax shook his head as the lightning flashed again. Nothing around that man seemed to faze him. Not once did he flinch.

Ajax finally made it to his feet. He had no clue what was going on.

"Hey, ass hat. What the hell are you doing!"

The man smiled and lifted his hand, lifting Ajax off his feet and moving him closer. This stunned Ajax into silence.

"Ajax. I like the ring of your name," the man said. "Are you ready to come home?"

Ajax squinted his eyes, unsure of what he was talking about. When Ajax tried to speak, the man closed his other hand. Ajax's throat closed. Ajax started to panic, but couldn't move or speak. The man laughed a thunderous, guttural laugh, as thunder boomed outside. He waved his hand, and Ajax went flying into the wall, and down into the broken glass. Ajax felt the glass penetrate his body.

Now, he was able to move, and his vocal cords seemed to be working. Ajax let out a growl of pain.

The man stood there, still laughing at the mess he'd made. The sight of Ajax's blood seemed to make him all the happier.

"Dantanian! Stop!" Quinn screamed.

Her scream was powerful enough to stop Dantanian's laugh, and the storm outside ended abruptly.

"Leave us now!" She said, this time not so loudly.

Dantanian cocked his head, and grinned his evil grin.

"You stuck around? I thought, after what I did to you, you would have bolted."

"Leave," Quinn repeated, her voice low, but harsh.

Dantanian laughed.

Quinn walked slowly toward him. In the background, she could hear Ajax telling her to "Get out! Run!"

She knew she couldn't do that.

Dantanian looked amused. He lifted his hand, and brought her closer to him. He placed his hands on her shoulders.

"So, angel, you must want me. You're still here, and asking for more."

He rubbed his hands up and down her shoulders.

"I might just trade you for him."

This time, Quinn smirked.

"I'm not a fool, Dantanian. My soul will never be yours. Want to know how I know?" Quinn waited.

Dantanian squinted his evil, black eyes.

"How's that, darling?" he asked, moving his face closer to hers. Dantanian was so close, he could taste her soul, and would have loved for her to be his queen.

"I know someone much more powerful, who says I belong to him."

Dantanian's expression turned to disgust, and then he back-handed Quinn; it knocked her a good four feet away.

Ajax, now numb to the pain, bolted at Dantanian. Dantanian was full of anger. With a flick of a finger, he stopped Ajax in his tracks.

"Don't worry. I won't toss you this time." Dantanian scooted Ajax back, and pinned him to the wall with his powers.

" I want you to watch. Such innocence, and a free pass to the gates above. Once I'm done with her, she'll have a one way ticket to hell, as my Queen."

Ajax fought against the elemental power holding him, but couldn't get free anytime soon.

Dantanian walked across the room, and lifted Quinn up by the back of her neck. Quinn slapped his hand away.

"You disgust me, you vile demon," Quinn spat.

"Oh, I like the pet name you have chosen for me," Dantanian said, with lust dripping from his words. He grabbed the back of Quinn's hair, and yanked her to the wall next to Ajax. Dantanian made sure she was almost close enough for them to touch. He knew it would drive Ajax crazy that she was right there, and he couldn't save her from what Dantanian was about to do.

"So, Ajax.   You still haven't scored?" Dantanian said, smiling at Ajax.

"Don't touch her!" Ajax growled in frustration.

Dantanian just smiled at him, and licked his lips.

"Look harder, Ajax."

When Dantanian smiled at him, it was like he was messing with his head. Ajax's mind started flashing, as he watched what was happening to Quinn. She looked as if she was enjoying it, and even participating. His gut turned, and anger crept in. Ajax blinked his eyes a few times, and the scene changed back to reality. Ajax growled in anger, but the more he fought, the tighter the hold became.

Quinn cringed, when the demon's mouth landed on hers. She held her breath, as he licked and traced her lips with his tongue. The more she squirmed and screamed under her breath, the more he seemed to enjoy it. Quinn closed her eyes, and prayed.

"Father, if you can hear me right now, I need your help. Please send me strength and courage to free myself from this evil. Please hear my prayer. Please hear my prayer. Please hear…"

Quinn was pulled from her prayer when pain invaded her mind.   When her eyes opened, Dantanian was using his finger to burn her shirt off of her. Quinn screamed in agony. As he was cutting the fabric, his lips followed the trail. Even his lips felt like jagged glass.   When he was halfway down, the pain was excruciating. Quinn was pulled into darkness, and the pain stopped.

"Quinn, calm your soul. We heard your prayer."

It was the angel, Michael's voice.

"You have the strength and courage you asked for. Use what has been given to you, and send his soul back to hell."

Pain jolted Quinn back to reality, and she let out a searing scream, which would have sent chills down anyone's spine. Her eyes focused, and she noticed her shirt lying at Ajax's feet. She looked up at Ajax. His eyes were so angry. Quinn nodded at him, and a tear ran down her cheek.

"It's okay."

Ajax's face showed that he didn't believe what she was saying. Ajax still fought against the force holding him.

"Dantanian," Quinn whispered, out of breath.

"Mmm. Yes, my darlin?" he whispered, in a gross, sexy voice, still kissing her neck with what felt like razor blades.

"You can't do this to me," Quinn whimpered through the pain.

He came up to look her in the eyes.

"To me, it seems I've already started. I'll have you both real soon."

"No," Quinn calmly said.

"There isn't anything you can do, child, but lay back and enjoy," Dantanian said, in a faked loving voice.

Quinn raised her hand to the side of his face and calmly looked into his eyes. Dantanian thought she was starting to give in to him, and he smiled and kissed her lips. Quinn opened up to his kiss and relaxed her body. This time, his lips didn't hurt her. It felt as it would have felt to kiss any other man. She wished he wasn't her first. Quinn let him kiss her for a moment, before she jammed the wooden crucifix, which held holy water, under his chin.

His eyes held shock, and maybe hurt? He yelled angrily.

"'Cause this is my world, not yours," Quinn said, just before he disappeared in black, powdery smoke.

Chapter 22

Quinn and Ajax both fell to the floor. When Quinn regained her awareness, she noticed that Ajax was bleeding. She didn't know how badly, but he had some pieces of glass sticking out of his upper arm, and from his legs. None seem to be in too deep. She grabbed her shirt, which was lying on the floor, and crawled over to him. With shaky hands, she lightly ran her hand down his face.

"You okay," he asked, a little winded.

Quinn didn't respond.

"Deep breath," she said to him.

When he took a deep breath, she pulled a sliver of glass from his upper arm. Ajax didn't seem to mind. He just looked at her calmly.

"That seemed to be the deepest," she explained.

She took her discarded shirt, and tied it around his arm to stop the bleeding.

"Be right back."

Quinn ran to the bathroom, and grabbed the first aid kit and some wet cloths. She dropped them down by Ajax, went into the kitchen, and grabbed a six-pack of beer out of the fridge. She walked back over, and sat cross-legged on the floor in front of Ajax. She opened a can of beer, and handed it to him.

"Mmm, thanks," he said, taking a long drink.

Quinn cracked open another. Ajax placed his hand on hers.

"You can't drink."

Quinn shrugged, and took a drink.

"I'll keep that in mind, next time," she said.

Ajax sat up a little, against the wall, smiled, and shook his head.

Quinn finished the whole can, and then took out the rest of the glass. All the other pieces were just slivers. She just cleaned the cuts, and put bandages over them.

"I don't wanna sound like a creep, and stuff, 'cause you're in your bra, but we should clean that red welt," Ajax said, trying not to smile.

Quinn didn't even blush this time. She grabbed two more beers, and opened them. She took a long drink from one, and gave him the other.

"It's fine. I think I'll live. Doesn't burn anymore, just looks bad. When I regain the energy, I'll go get another shirt, so creep all you want."

Ajax laughed.

"We shouldn't be laughing," he said.

Quinn looked at the door, and then back at him.

"We should be lucky that we can still laugh. We're not dead, yet."

Ajax sighed. "Come here."

Quinn scooted closer, and leaned on his good arm.

"He's a demon, or the devil himself; I don't know. When, and if, he comes back, we won't be so lucky."

Ajax kissed the top of her head.

"Let's hope we don't see him for a long while, then."

Quinn nodded and wrapped her arms around Ajax's good arm.

Ajax sat with Quinn, in silence, as they drank their beers. His mind was going through what had just happened, from start to finish. He was tossed around, but nothing hurt him more than when Quinn allowed Dantanian to kiss her, and she responded to him. He wasn't sure whether she was enjoying it or not, but he hoped she didn't. He hates himself for feeling that way, but he hadn't even got that far with her. He brought his mostly full beer to his lips, and drained the can, without stopping until there wasn't a drop left. He was starting to feel a lot better than he had a half hour ago, and a lot wiser.

"So, all this crap is real, huh?" Ajax said, in a deep voice.

"Yeah, it's been real for me for a long time," Quinn replied.

Ajax wiggled out of her hold, and turned toward her.

"Ever been that close with him before?"

Quinn looked up at him.

"Only when he's in my dream."

"So he can reach you here, or in your dreams?" Ajax asked, his voice raised a bit.

Quinn wasn't sure what he was asking, or if he was asking her at all.

"Well?" he huffed.

"Yes, looks like he can," Quinn said, confused. "What's wrong? Are you angry with me?" she added, still very confused, and not quite shocked.

"I wouldn't say I was mad, I'd say I'm just a little pissed!" Ajax raised his voice a little more.

Quinn stood up.

"Tonight was a lot to take in. I'll give you some space, so take it easy."

Quinn walked down the hall, and to the bedroom. Quinn undressed, down to her underwear. She opened the dresser, and grabbed a tank and pajama shorts; she pulled the tank over her head. When she turned around, to grab her shorts, Ajax was leaning against the door jamb, staring at her. He didn't look angry, at the moment; he looked sad or hurt.

"Did you enjoy it?" he asked.

Quinn looked at him, puzzled, but didn't want to make his mood worse.

He came into the room, and leaned his back against the wall, facing Quinn.

Quinn closed the distance by a few feet.

"I'm scared to anger you. If you want to know if I enjoyed what happened tonight, then no. I wouldn't say being mauled by a demon is something I enjoy."

Ajax curled his lips in disgust.

"Don't pretend nothing happened! You let him kiss you, and you went along with it willingly. You didn't stop it, like you did at first. Why? Because you did enjoy it!"

Quinn quickly wiped away tears that had escaped her eyes.

"Fine, Ajax, I did enjoy it.'

Ajax stepped forward in disbelief, thinking maybe he heard her wrong.

Quinn's voice was shaky when she spoke.

"I enjoyed it, 'cause when I stopped struggling, the pain went away. Have you ever been burned by hell's fire?"

Quinn took a second to keep from falling apart.

"When hell's fire is burning you, you can't think of anything but how much you want to die. Letting him kiss me, it gave me a clear head. That's how I was able to listen to…"

Quinn looked up at Ajax. He looked completely normal. Quinn heard a voice in her mind.

"Ajax was made to see so much more than what happened. He knows this now."

Quinn walked up to Ajax.

"It's not your fault; he put this in your mind, trying to turn us from each other, and to make it painful for you."

Ajax nodded his head, and a tear escaped.

"I would never raise my voice to you like that. Oh, Lord. I don't understand what's happening...."

Ajax took a second to gather his true thoughts.

"I remember everything the way it happened, but a few minutes ago, it was so much more. He was all over you, and you were loving it."

Quinn looked up at him. "I'm sorry. If I had a choice, this wouldn't have happened to you at all. I'm sorry he could mess with your head."

She wrapped her arms around his waist. After a moment, he melted into her. He held her for a long while.

"I'm so sorry," he whispered.

"Me, too."

After what felt like forever, Ajax let go of Quinn.

"Can we sleep? We can talk more, and clean up, in the morning."

Quinn smiled. "Yeah, I'll go shut the door." She walked over to the dresser, and put her shorts on.

"Nice undies," Ajax said, trying to laugh during a yawn.

"Shut up and sleep."

When Quinn came back from locking up, Ajax was already asleep. She crawled into her own bed, and fell fast asleep.

Chapter 23

"Hell's. Fire. Is. Debilitating.

"There's no other pain like it. Physical and mental anguish. When hell's fire is even close to you, all you can think of is how nice death would be at that moment. I've never in my life wished I were dead, until he came close to me, and touched me with hell's fire.

"You know how my car went off into the water? I can never get that chill out of my bones? Hell's fire's like that; even if it's not being used, I can feel it burning deep inside my bones. From time to time, I can feel the burn of the cold and the burn of hell's fire at the same time.

"That's just the physical part. The psychological part makes you so scared. The fear overcomes your mind. Your mind and heart have never felt this much pain, and never knew they could. Around all that pain, somehow, loneliness and despair, and a feeling of smothering seeps into your mind. Hell can play with your mind. It did a job on Ajax's last night. It changed him into someone different. It was scary to see him act the way he did. It wasn't him but, somehow, he fought it."

Father David listened intently. When Quinn finished speaking, he wiped the mist from his eyes.

"What do you feel or see on the other side, when you're in God's land?"

"That's so hard to describe, Father David. It's something you have to feel and see to believe. I'll try my best to describe it for you, though. When you reach heaven, every ache, every pain, and every mental anguish that you have ever felt disappears. Nothing is erased, just the emotions that are attached to it. Like I'll be able to remember what happened to me last night, but I won't hurt from it, like I do now. Like I will for the rest of my life. You could feel the love radiating from the air that you take in, or you think you're taking in. I imagine it would be like being in the womb again: someone always taking care of you, loving you, nurturing you, and giving you everything you ever needed. That's not even a small part that I can describe. It would be so impossible to tell you exactly what it's like. One day, you'll see for yourself. Let's pray it's a long time from now, though. You still have so much to do."

Father David nodded his head. His emotions were guarded well.

"How do you know all this?"

Quinn put her hand in his, and he gave it a squeeze.

"I receive messages," Quinn smiled. "Ever since the accident. At first, I thought I was going crazy," Quinn added.

"Is there anything else you want to tell me?"

Quinn wiped away tears that were streaming down her cheek.

"Oh, there's so much more I want to tell you, but I can't. I can't cause the outcome to change," Quinn said.

Father David put his hands on each side of her face.

"You know how this whole thing is going to end?"

"Father, it's not as bad as you fear."

After a few minutes, Father David nodded, but still thought the future was just as bad as he thought, and that Quinn was downplaying it.

"How's Ajax handling it?"

Quinn stood up, and took a sip of her coffee.

"Surprisingly, better than me. He's seen so much, and he's still here. If the roles were reversed, I'm not sure I would be."

Quinn refilled their mugs, and sat down again.

"Quinn, I know you would be. You have a knack for helping anyone in need. God chose you, because you're brave and have the purest loving heart."

In the back of the cabin, Ajax lay in bed, and listened to everything. He didn't hear when the Father arrived. He woke up just as she was explaining her experience with hell and its fire. He didn't realize how painful everything was. He knew it was bad, but she never let on how awful it really was. It took Father David to get it out of her, and even then, she wasn't telling him everything.

Quinn had told him last night, but it didn't sink in until then. Ajax wiped the sleep from his eyes, and grabbed a clean shirt out of the night stand.

"Mornin'," Ajax said, entering the room. He walked over and shook Father David's hand.

"I'm relieved that you're here, Father. It was a rough night."

"I've heard," Father David replied.

Quinn walked up and placed a hand on Ajax's back, reached around, and gave him a cup of coffee. Ajax took the mug, but grabbed her hand with his free hand.

"You feel alright?"

Quinn smiled tightly, and nodded.

Ajax winked. "Liar."

That made Quinn smile. Ajax still held on to her, and they looked at each other for a long moment. They shared in a moment of eye contact and understanding, which left them in a happier state than they'd just been in.

"Father David, would you take a walk with me, down to the lake?" Ajax asked.

Father David stood up, and walked over to the door.

"Sure, Son, I could use a little fresh air right about now."

As they walked, Ajax just had to ask.

"Father, I was baptized as a baby. I haven't had confession since I was eight. My mom taught me one thing, and my dad did everything to undo everything she worked hard to do." Ajax paused for a minute, and Father David let him gather his thoughts.

"Father, my eyes opened last night. If that's anything like hell's gonna be, I really don't wanna go there. I have a feeling that the path I lead when I was younger has me one foot in already. Can we change my path?"

When they reached the dock, Father David sat down on the edge.

"I don't believe you're destined for hell, Ajax. If you'd like to do confession, we can do it right here, right now. I'll help you through this, as I do all God's children."

Father David pulled a long piece of wide, purple ribbon out of his pocket. When he draped it around his neck, Ajax saw that it was a stole for confessions. Ajax and Father David stayed on the dock for a long while. Ajax gave his confession, and they prayed together for the longest time. During a silent prayer, Ajax prayed mostly for Quinn. He prayed that she would never have to go through anything like last night again. He prayed for compassion, forgiveness, and strength to protect Quinn. His prayers were so pure and selfless: Ajax could feel God's presence. Ajax had felt this before: just last night, when he wasn't himself. God helped him fight hell's doing.

Chapter 24

After dinner, Father David joined Quinn and Ajax on the porch, to enjoy coffee. The porch was large, and wrapped around the whole cabin. It was a beautiful evening, and the sun was still midway in the sky, and reflecting off the lake. The smell of pine was strong and sweet. There was a gentle breeze, which made the warm evening very relaxing.

Father David sat on an oversized wooden rocker, with his eyes closed lightly, enjoying the warmth on his face. Quinn sat cross-legged, with her back to the wooden railing, sipping her coffee. Ajax sat in the other large rocker, with his eyes mostly on Quinn. After about ten minutes, Quinn broke the silence.

"Father David, with everything going on, do you think it'd be safer if Ajax and I went different ways until this is over?"

Ajax sat up a little, peeved at her question.

"Ajax, don't look at me like that. I mean you have a real person after you, something you can avoid. Why would you wanna get involved with the Devil?" Quinn said, showing no emotion.

Ajax, still a little red in the face, countered here question. "I do believe I'm already involved. I'm not going anywhere, and you're as..." Ajax fixed his wording. "Butt's not going anywhere without me."

Quinn remained calm.

"I don't wanna be anywhere you're not, but think about how much safer you'd be, just moving."

Ajax stood up and paced back and forth, from one side of the porch to the other. Father David just watched in wonder, and a little amusement. When Ajax made his way back to the side where he'd started, he sat down, facing Quinn.

"No," was all he said.

"You're a stubborn man! A pig-headed, stubborn man! You're actin' a fool right now!" Quinn said, annoyed, but not angry.

"Well, isn't that the pot calling the kettle black?" Ajax shot back.

After a few moments of them on a stare-down, Ajax softened his face.

"Look, if I thought leaving you would make you safe, I'd do it in a heartbeat. I know you're doing this to keep me safe. I'm sorry, I'd rather be here with you, than safe somewhere else and alone, worrying about you. If you can't see how I feel, I'm doing something wrong."

Quinn didn't do anything about the tears that escaped her eyes. Ajax reached over and wiped one off her cheek with his thumb. Quinn leaned into his hand.

"No, you're doing it right," she said, with a wink. "I think."

Father David clapped his hands loudly. "Okay, kids, I almost thought I was in couples counseling for a minute there. You fixed it all by yourselves; that's huge, all in itself." Father David stood up.

"I guess I should be going. I wanna stop by Adam and Eve's before heading back home. Quinn, I have your mother's letter; I'll give her it first thing in the morning. Ajax, I'll give your mom the message you asked me to."

Everyone said their goodbyes, and Quinn and Ajax waved until they could no longer see the car.

"I'm not sorry," Quinn said, standing in the middle of the driveway.

"Neither am I," Ajax responded.

Ajax walked closer, and held his hand out; Quinn took it.

"The only thing I'm sorry for isn't meeting you sooner. Not being with you when you needed someone, after your car accident."

Quinn took a step toward Ajax.

"You didn't know me."

Ajax matched her, and took another step in, too.

"No, I didn't, and I'm sorry for that, too. Something brought me here, to you. Is it possible this is God's doing?"

Quinn smiled.

"He does work in mysterious ways."

Ajax gently pulled her closer to him, enough that Quinn could smell his aftershave. She stared at his chest a moment. For some reason, she was nervous, and her insides were shaking, and the butterflies were making flutter in her belly. She could feel his warm breath on the top of her head. Slowly, she looked up, to meet his stare. Neither moved for the longest time.

Ajax's breath was a little faster. The way she looked at him was driving him crazy,: something he'd never felt before. He could tell she was nervous; her hand was shaking in his. Ajax waited before he made any movement. When her hands stopped shaking, he placed a small kiss on her forehead. Ajax felt Quinn squeeze his hand. She looked up at him, and smiled. Ajax moved in a little more, leaving no space between them. Quinn was tense for a moment, but then relaxed. She leaned her head up in approval.

Ajax noticed, but didn't want to rush. He was enjoying himself. He leaned down, and pecked the tip of her nose. Quinn let go of his hand, and grabbed the side of his shirt. They were so close, it made her balance unsteady.

Ajax's eyes never left hers. He took his newly freed hands, and brushed her heavy locks behind her shoulders. He slowly and softly ran his left hand down her left side. If Quinn wasn't so into this, she would have laughed, because it tickled. He put his right hand on the back of her neck, and paused. Quinn smiled, stood on her toes, and placed a few kisses on his stubbly chin. It took

Ajax everything he had to stay cool and steady. He smiled down at her, and put his right hand in the back of her hair, giving it a little tug to lift her face to the sky. This made Quinn inhale quickly. Ajax bent down, and trailed kisses along her jaw line. Ajax felt the quickening of her breath, and she gripped his side now, not his shirt. He pulled her closer, with his left hand on her hip. He could feel the heat radiating off her body. He moved his left hand up the middle of her back, under her shirt. Quinn shivered, because he was doing it so slowly. He tilted her head back some more, and traced kisses from her chin to her ear.

They were both breathing heavily now. Quinn moved her arms to his shoulders, and pushed him back a little. Ajax was a little worried, until she pulled his face down, and pressed his closed lips to hers. Just as they were parting their lips for a deeper kiss, thunder boomed, and hail and rain fell from the sky, hard and fast.

Ajax scooped Quinn up, and she wrapped her legs around his waist; he quickly got them to the porch. Quinn still wrapped tightly around him, he placed her back against the door of the house. Quinn was higher than she was moments ago. She placed a kiss on his forehead. Her arms tight around his neck, he buried his head in her collarbone, and breathed in her scent. He slowly ran his lips across the dip of her neck to her collarbone and that made a little moan escape Quinn's lips. She pulled his head back and gave him a sweet kiss: one, two, and then three.

His whole body told him to take her to bed, but something told him not to go any further. Ajax lightly kissed her back. Nose to nose, he took a deep breath.

"This is so very, very painful for me to say, but I think we should slow down, just a bit."

Quinn looked into his eyes. She saw nothing but want, so she knew he still wanted her; the rejection didn't hurt her. She gave him another kiss, and he kissed her back.

"Okay, maybe a good idea," Quinn agreed.

Ajax let out a growl of frustration.

"I'm sorry," Quinn whispered.

"Not as much as I am," he replied, with a dramatic pout.

Quinn giggled at his response. She loosened her legs, and slowly slid down his body. He was still holding her close, very close.

"You're making this so much harder," Quinn teased.

Ajax bit down on his bottom lip, trying to calm his insides.

Quinn leaned up, and kissed him quickly. Ajax moved back about an inch.

"Will food help?" Quinn asked.

"Pie. Pie will help," Ajax replied, with a sexy smile and a wink.

Chapter 25

When Ajax rolled out of bed in the morning, Quinn was still sound asleep, in the fetal position. This had to be the only night she had slept without any issues. They'd gone to bed before nine at night, and it was already eight in the morning. Ajax showered and dressed. When he came out, she was still asleep.

"Maybe I'll try my hand at breakfast; if all else fails, I know how to make coffee and toast," he thought.

Ajax tried making scrambled eggs, but failed. He dumped the eggs in the trash, and scrubbed the burn-on eggs out of the pan. He poured a cup of coffee, and took it to the porch, where he sat in the warm sun.

His mind went back to when his lips were on Quinn's. So close, but yet so far away. Just thinking about it made him break out in goose bumps. Ajax really didn't want to screw this up. He never really tried not to before. He was happy with failing any time.

"Not this time," he whispered.   "After all that's going on, my mind's always on her. You'd think, when hell is really breaking loose, that people wouldn't be falling for someone, when the world seems to be falling in on itself."

A little after eleven, Quinn woke up. She lay in bed, feeling perfectly rested. The bed across the room was empty, and already made up. She closed her eyes, and went over her dream in her head, to make sure she didn't miss anything. She dreamt that she was sitting on a park bench, in the same place she always met Michael. They sat and talked about what was to come. Michael told her she had two paths she could take, and none of them were wrong; either way she chose, her soul would remain clean. It was up to her to make the decision of which path she would take, when the time came. He also told her the love she felt for Ajax was real, as was his was for her.

Quinn made her bed, grabbed clean clothes, and jumped into the shower. The hot water felt great, as it landed on her body. It was like a water massage. She took her time, and relaxed, soaking up the steam the hot water provided.

Her mind drew her back to yesterday, when she kissed Ajax. She put her finger on her lips, as she remembered. His kisses lingered until the time she fell asleep. They both went to bed early, scared of what they would do if they stayed awake any longer. Temptation was on high yesterday. Quinn wondered whether it was his sweet words or his kiss. Quinn smiled,

"Both," she said to herself.

Quinn dressed, and brushed her teeth in a rush. She spent way too much time in the shower. She was starving, and in need of some coffee. She made her way to the kitchen. Ajax was nowhere in the house. She opened the fridge, and leaned in. They seemed to be out of almost everything.

"We'll just have to run to Adam and Eve's later," she thought.

Quinn closed the fridge, turned, and about jumped out of her skin. Ajax stood right behind her, smiling, and holding two mugs of coffee.

He handed her a mug without saying a thing, and then he leaned in, and gave her a sweet, dry kiss.

"You didn't even hear me come in, or pour the coffee?" Ajax asked, smiling.

"My mind's been elsewhere," Quinn replied, blushing a little.

Ajax was pleased that she was thinking about the same thing he was thinking.

"Uh huh, and what might that be?" he teased.

Quinn blushed deeper.

"If we continue this right now, I'm not sure if it'll end as well as yesterday," Quinn confessed.

Ajax raised his eyebrows in surprise, and seemed proud of himself.

"Okay, I'll take you on your word," Ajax replied, and then added, "There's a little town not too far away. Why don't I take you to dinner?"

Quinn smiled.

"You askin' me out?" Quinn asked, smiling.

"Yep, or we can stay here, and see how much trouble we can get into?" Ajax teased.

"Dinner it is," Quinn said quickly.

The drive wasn't as long as she expected. The town wasn't much bigger than the one they were staying in, although this one did have a diner, a drive-through joint, a gas station, and a one-stop shop called Al's Shop All.

Ajax pulled up in front of the dinner. He jumped out, as Quinn grabbed her shawl and wallet. Ajax opened her door, and offered his arm. Quinn accepted, with a smile. Ajax shut the door, and led her into the diner. The place smelled so good. The interior was outdated. They had orange booths, and a jukebox in the corner. On the far end was a bar, with stools that went from one end to the other. The stools were the same orange as the booths. The floor was black and white checked tiles. The lighting wasn't too bright. They had lamps that hung from the ceiling, and matched the color of the checkered flooring. The diner looked like it was the popular spot in town; it seemed almost everyone was there.

Ajax guided her to an empty booth in the corner. He sat with his back to the wall, and Quinn sat across from him. They looked at the menus for a moment, before a very pretty waitress approached to take their order. She had naturally red hair, which was straight, long, and hung in a braid down her back. Her eyes were green, and her lips were painted lush red.

"What can I get you?" she asked, looking right at Ajax, while batting her eyes, and sticking out her hip.

Ajax looked at Quinn.

"What are you getting?"

"I'll have the ribs."

Ajax raised his brows and smiled.

"What? I'm starving," Quinn said, smiling.

"And you, hun?" The waitress asked, still batting her eyes at Ajax.

"Make that two rib dinners and two Cokes," Ajax replied.

The waitress made her way back to the bar very slowly, working her walk. Quinn discreetly rolled her eyes.

Ajax reached over, and held Quinn's hand. She covered his hand with her other hand. They sat there, holding hands, and looking at each other. They didn't say anything; they didn't have to. They would have sat even longer, if the sound of a throat clearing didn't break their moment. It was the waitress. She set down Quinn's plate without even acknowledging Quinn was there. She leaned down to place Ajax's plate on the table.

"Anything else I can get you, honey?" she asked in a sweet voice.

Ajax smiled at her, his very hot smile.

"Yes, there is. Could you do me the biggest favor, and make sure no one else comes over here, unless we call? See, this beautiful lady and I are on our first real date. I'd really like to finish this meal, and take her home, so we can get to know each other a little more."

The waitress stood up stiffly. Her flirting side was completely gone.

"Yeah, whatever," she said, and stomped away.

Quinn raised her eyebrows at Ajax.

"What're you planning?"

Ajax laughed.

"She's gone, right? That was my plan. That was getting annoying," Ajax replied.

The dinner went without a hitch. They both cleared their plates, and couldn't move for a few minutes. They were both so full. Ajax left plenty of money on the table to cover dinner and a tip. He grabbed Quinn's hand, and led her out of the diner to the car, where he opened the door, so she could climb in. He climbed in the other side, and started the car, but didn't start driving.

"Something wrong?" Quinn asked.

"Yeah, there's something I need to do," he said.

Before Quinn could ask, he pulled her into another long, dry kiss. When he pulled back, Quinn was flushed.

"Much better," he said, pulling out onto the road.

Quinn was still recovering from the kiss.

When they got back to town they dropped in on Adam and Eve's for some things needed at the cabin. It was late, so they didn't stay very long, but Quinn invited them over for dinner the following night. They both seemed to be happy, and Eve was still in good spirits.

The sun had just gone down when they made it back to the cabin. They unloaded everything, and put it all away. They were still uncomfortably full and tired. Quinn went and used the bathroom, and brushed her teeth. When she came out, Ajax went in with his night pants in his hands. Quinn changed quickly into her shorts and tank pajamas. As Ajax was coming out, Quinn was putting away her cloths. Ajax walked up and pulled her into a soft hug. She laid her face on his chest, and listened to his heart beating slowly and smoothly, unlike her heart at the moment. Quinn pulled her head away from his body, and looked up at him. Ajax's face was calm and relaxed. Quinn reached up and pecked his lips softly, and he returned it just the same as she gave.

"Thanks for an awesome first date," Quinn whispered.

Ajax closed his eyes and smiled.

"Thank you for going, not rejecting the offer."

Quinn smiled.

"I'd have been a fool to reject you."

After a few moments of embrace, they went to their beds, and shut off the lights; they both lay there, wondering what the other was thinking, until sleep invaded them both.

Chapter 26

The sky was dark, and the air around her smelled of something foul burning. Quinn turned in a circle, and there was nothing but emptiness surrounding her. The air was thick, and burned he chest when she breathed in. She knew where she was.

"I'm in Hell," she whispered, as a shiver tore down her spine. Quinn waited for a while to see whether something would show up, or whether she could will herself out of there. She reached for her neck, and the necklace wasn't there.

When she failed at thinking her way out, she started walking. In what direction, she didn't know. Everything looked exactly the same, no matter which way she turned. She walked and walked, until she became winded; that didn't take long: the burning in her chest didn't help matters much. When she caught her breath, she started walking again. The ground was packed dirt and ash, and when she took a step, the ash blew up around her. In the distance, she saw what looked like a long building. She picked up her pace, in hope that this might be her way out.

The building was black, with silver trim. Quinn pulled the door handle, shrieked, and let go. The door was as hot as fire. She pulled her hands up to examine, and they were very red, with a layer or two of skin gone. After calming herself from the pain, she pulled her shirt over her head, leaving her in her sports bra. She wrapped her shirt around one hand, as thickly as she could, on her palm. She pulled the handle with all her strength, and the door opened. She didn't waste any time getting inside. If she thought it was hot outside, inside was so much hotter. Sweat just rolled down, like it would if she was in the shower. She unwrapped the shirt from her in hand, ripped it in two, and wrapped both hands, which were still throbbing in pain.

Quinn wiped the sweat from her eyes, and looked up. She was staring down a hallway. There was nothing there, except a door every 15 feet or so. Every door looked the same. There were no numbers or words to tell them apart, nor any door knobs. She started walking. When she reached the first door, she wasn't going to try to touch it. She learned her lesson the first time. She used her foot, and kicked it open. As soon as she opened it, screams pierced her ear. The sound was so debilitating that she dropped to her knees, with her hands over her ears. When she thought she was losing her mind, the door slammed in her face, leaving her a mess on the hot, ashy floor.

Gathering herself, she walked farther down the hall. This time, she wasn't going to just pick any door. She was going to use her senses. She walked and walked, until she felt something deep inside. She kicked the door open, and saw blackness, with fire burning up from the floor. Not a second later, the door slammed on her again. This time, there was something written on the door, which read, "Ajax: Human soul burns here."

Quinn stumbled back, gasping for air that left her body from the shock. She couldn't cry; there was no water left in her body.

Quinn started walking again, but much slower. Her energy was draining fast. The heat was just killing her slowly. After walking for what seemed forever, she got a feeling deep inside again. She turned to the right; another door faced her, which looked the same as the last hundreds. She kicked it open; what was there was anything but darkness. Her eyes squinted at the sun, which was just about to go down. Everything was green, and a cool breeze moved the trees. Quinn stepped into the room, not caring what could happen if she did. She stepped through, and nothing happened. The cool breeze felt heavenly on her face. It was late evening, wherever she was. The sun was slowly setting, and wildlife scurried to find a place to hide for the night. In the distance, Quinn heard water, but she was no longer thirsty. Time seemed to be going much faster, because the sky was getting darker, and the sun moving below the earth. Then everything went silent.

Quinn stood still, listening. She could hear fast movement coming from the opposite direction. She did a double take when she saw herself and Ajax, hand in hand, running as fast as they could. A loud bang sounded, and everything slowed down. Ajax let go of Quinn, and pushed her to the ground. As he did, Ajax stumbled and fell. The Quinn watching everything screamed at them to get up, but only the Quinn stood up on shaky legs, and ran to Ajax. Her mouth was moving, but Quinn couldn't hear anything. She saw her roll him over, but Ajax was dead. His eyes were wide open, facing up to the dark sky. Both Quinns screamed in agony, but her own was the only scream she could hear.

Suddenly, she was jerked out of Hell, and landed softly in a field of green. All her pain disappeared as soon as her feet touched the luscious grass.

"Michael," she called in her mind.

"I am here, child. I brought you here. I wanted you to know that what you saw wasn't fate, but what the demons wanted you to see."

Quinn listened closely to everything he said. Michael's voice was music to her ears, and calmed her soul. Michael spoke for a while before bidding her farewell.

Quinn lingered in the beautiful grass before she forced herself to leave. She lay down and closed her eyes, and then felt her body drift down.

"Quinn, can you hear me?" a familiar voice asked

Quinn's eyes felt heavy, and her body was so very achy, like she had the flu. She tried to open her eyes again, but she just couldn't.

"Ajax," she heard the familiar voice again.

"It's Eve. Oh, Eve, I'm here," Quinn thought.

"I think she's trying to wake up," Eve said.

Quinn felt a movement that shot pain through her body, and then soft lips touched her forehead.

"Her fever is gone, thank God."

Quinn tried again to open her eyes to Ajax's voice. Again, she failed.

"Quinn?"

Ajax was whispering in her ear.

"If you can hear me, please squeeze my hand."

Quinn felt Ajax place his hand in hers. His hand felt so cool; it felt so good.

"Quinn, please squeeze."

Quinn gathered all her strength, and squeezed.

"Did you see that? She squeezed pretty hard."

Ajax whispered in her ear again, "Maybe your mind needs more rest. Sleep, Quinn, and then wake up to me."

Quinn felt so much emotion.

"Eve, look, tears," Ajax said in a low voice.

Ajax stayed and spoke softly in her ear for the longest time. Quinn didn't hear everything; she was falling back to sleep.

When Quinn woke up again, she didn't try to open her eyes right away. Everything was so quiet. She felt something hard beside her, and heard soft breathing. She tried moving her hands.

They moved. She felt around, and grabbed what she was hoping was a hand.

"Quinn," Ajax said softly. He leaned over, and did something on the other side of her.

"Quinn, can you open your eyes?" Ajax whispered.

Quinn relaxed her body, and willed her eyes to open. They fluttered, and then shut again.

"Yes, that's great, you're doing great," Ajax said encouragingly.

Quinn tried again, but with every fiber of her being. Again, they fluttered, but opened, not too wide, but just enough to make out a blurred Ajax.

"Hey, there you are," Ajax said, trailing soft kisses all over her forehead.

Quinn squinted, and that made Ajax lean over her again; the pain in her eyes went away. She opened them all the way this time. She was about to talk, but her mouth was so dry, she couldn't even move her tongue. Ajax noticed and held a cup of ice water to her lips. Quinn took a few long drinks, and lay back again. They had her propped up with tons of pillows.

"Hey," Quinn said, looking right at Ajax.

"Hey, back at ya," he replied.

"I was dreaming," Quinn said.

"You don't remember anything but the dream? Ajax asked.

Quinn shook her head, and put her hand in his. Quinn felt so tired all of a sudden.

"Can we sleep? I promise we can talk more tomorrow."

Ajax nodded, kissed her softly on the lips, reached over, and shut off the light.

As Quinn was drifting off to sleep, she could feel Ajax's arm tighten around her. His face was so close to her, she could feel his sweet breath on her cheek. He used his other hand to rub her forehead, right below her hairline. With everything he was doing, Quinn fell fast asleep.

Chapter 27

Quinn woke up with the sun.   Ajax was already awake, watching her.

"Good morning," she said, smiling.

"Mornin'," Ajax replied.

Ajax looked as though he hadn't slept at all.

"Did you sleep any?" Quinn asked.

"Very little," Ajax said.

Quinn sat up, and grabbed Ajax's hand.

"Come on, I'll fix us some breakfast."

Ajax willingly followed Quinn to the kitchen, and started the coffee, while she started breakfast. Quinn whipped up some fried eggs and sausage, and put them on biscuits. While she was taking them to the table, Ajax poured the coffee and a couple glasses of orange juice.

Sitting at the table, eating, Ajax just couldn't wait any longer to ask what he'd tried to ask last night.

"Do you remember anything?"

Quinn shook her head, "Not really."

Ajax drank down the rest of his juice, and pushed his plate away.

"You had the highest fever: over 107. You were freaking seizing on and off for hours. I used the emergency cell to call Adam. Eve checked you out, and said you were fine, except for the fever and the seizing."

Quinn pushed her plate away, and took a sip of her coffee.

"I don't think it was a medical fever, Ajax. I was in Hell."

Ajax slammed his mug down a little harder than he meant, and made Quinn jump.

"He didn't...," Ajax trailed off. He couldn't make the words come out.

It took Quinn a minute to understand what he was asking.

"No, I didn't see him, although, I know he was watching."

Ajax put his head in his hands, exhausted and a little relieved.

"I think the heat from Hell was affecting my body," Quinn thought out loud.

"Wanna tell me about it?" Ajax asked.

"How about this: I'll tell you everything, if you take a nap."

Ajax didn't object.

"I'll crash on the couch. Do me a favor and just don't leave the cabin till I'm up, okay?"

Quinn gathered the dishes, and put them in the sink. She walked behind where Ajax was sitting, and leaned in, giving him a kiss on the cheek.

"I promise," she whispered.

Quinn watched Ajax walk over to the couch and remove his shirt. As he put a sheet over the couch, she walked over to the sink, started the water, and watched the suds start to come live. As she picked up a dish, she felt Ajax's arms wrap around her waist; he set his chin on her shoulder, turned his head, and kissed her cheek.

"The last couple days have been so hard. Try not to ever leave me that long again. Not sure if I can cope without you. I know we haven't known each other that long, but I do know I love you with every fiber of my being."

Ajax didn't wait for a response. He kissed her once more, near the back of her ear, and squeezed her tight. When Ajax walked away, she wiped the secret tears away. She knew how he felt, because she felt it too. She didn't want to feel this, because she knew it could only end in pain. She'd seen it, felt it, and lived it multiple times.

After Quinn finished the dishes, she went and ran bath water, and added her bubble bath. While waiting for the tub to fill, she got her duffel bag from under the bed she slept in, and retrieved her father's handgun, which she'd brought along. Right by the window were the built-in closets and cabinets. She stood on the bunk bed ladder, and placed the weapon safely in the cabinet closest to the window.

"Just in case," she thought.

After soaking in the bath for over an hour, she dressed and headed out to the living room, where she pulled the Bible off the self. She sat down in front on the couch, where Ajax slept. She read for a long time, until the lighting in the room changed. Quinn looked up, and the sun was going down. She closed the book, and set it on her lap, tracing the beautiful engravings.

"The last page you read was something I remember hearing when I used to attend church with my mom, as a child," Ajax said from behind her.

Quinn hadn't realized he was awake. When he spoke, she could feel the heat from his breath on the back of her neck; that send chills down her spine.

"It's always been the page I go to most, when I need guidance," Quinn replied.

Quinn stood up, and placed the Bible back where it belonged. She stayed with her back to Ajax for a moment, and then walked over to him, still lying on the sofa, and sat on his upper legs.

"Oh, whatcha do that for," he asked, with half a deep laugh.

Quinn swallowed and took in a shaky breath.

Ajax squinted his eyes, not sure whether she should be worried. He sat up, and pulled her closer. Quinn could feel the warmth from his bare chest, and from his hands on her knees.

"Should I be worried?" Ajax asked.

Quinn closed her eyes, took in another shaky breath, and let it out.

"I love you, too," she said softly, and then quickly added, "Yes, I think we should be worried about this."

Ajax completely ignored the last part, and completely flipped them over. He was hovering over her; he leaned down, and planted kisses on every inch of her face.

"I'm not worried, not right now," Ajax said, looking into her eyes.

Ajax leaned in closer, and Quinn closed her eyes.

"Keep 'em open," Ajax requested.

Quinn opened her eyes, and Ajax came in slowly, and gave her a soft, dry kiss on the lips. Their eyes never left each other's.

"Why're you always a gentleman?" Quinn asked, after she leaned up some.

"What do you mean?" he asked, with a guttural laugh.

Quinn now felt a little embarrassed that she even asked.

"I mean, you most likely don't kiss me as you have others," she said, uncomfortable with the conversation she'd started.

Ajax raised up, and pulled her with him.

"You're right; I've kissed many girls."

Quinn looked away, really feeling out of place now. He turned her face back to him, and continued. "You're not those girls. I can't really explain it, but when the time's right, we'll both know, and we'll both enjoy it more than we ever have before."

Quinn felt uneasy. Ajax noticed and asked, "Why do you look worried? It's not like we haven't kissed anyone else before. I know you've had boyfriends," he said, half laughing.

"You're right, I've had a couple boyfriends," Quinn admitted.

"See, when we kiss, it'll be different than the last people we've kissed."

Quinn nodded. "Yeah, I guess you're right."

Quinn stood up, and made her way down the hall.

Ajax sat and thought for a few moments. "That was an odd conversation," he thought.

He went to the small bathroom, where he'd left his spare toothbrush; he had morning breath. As he brushed, a light bulb went off his head. "Oh, man! I didn't see that coming," he said to himself in the mirror.

He finished brushing as quickly as he could, and walked out of the bathroom. Quinn was walking down the hall toward him. Ajax stepped out in front of her.

"Hi," she said.

Ajax didn't say anything; he used his body to guide her, until her back was against the wall. Quinn didn't understand whether he was in his right mind at this point.

"Do me a favor?" Ajax asked.

Quinn nodded her head.

"Close your eyes, and don't move any part of your body."

Quinn looked at him questioningly.

"Don't worry, I haven't lost my mind," he said, smiling. "Please, for me, just close your eyes, and no matter what, don't move anything."

Quinn played along. She closed her eyes and completely relaxed her body.

Ajax watched her face relax. He leaned in, so she could feel his breath close. He watched her shoulders as she breathed. He put one hand on the wall next to her face, and the other hand softly on her cheek, and rubbed circles with his thumb. Ajax leaned in, and softly kissed her lips. Quinn moved her lips to mimic his.

"Don't move," he reminded.

Quinn took a shaky breath in and let it out. Her lips parted just a bit when she exhaled. Again, he leaned in, and landed a kiss softly on her lower lip. It took everything in him not to ruin the real thing. He opened his lips just enough to suck in a little bit of her upper lip. Her breathing caught in her chest. Ajax pressed her tight to the wall, know she was relaxing way too much. He kissed her upper lip again, and slipped his tongue out, only touching her upper lip, and then he planted a small, dry kiss in the same spot. He slowly moved his head away. After a moment, Quinn's eyes slowly opened.

"That's just a hint of a real kiss; when the time comes, and we both participate, it'll be so much better," Ajax whispered, a little winded.

"Wow," slipped out of her mouth.

Ajax laughed. "Yeah, wow."

"What was that for?" Quinn asked.

"Well, for some reason, I got the feeling you never truly kissed anyone."

Quinn smiled, a little embarrassed.

Ajax moved his weight off of Quinn, leaned in, and kissed her forehead.

"I'm really looking forward to our first," he said.

Quinn smiled.

"Come on, I'm hungry," she said, pulling him with her to the kitchen.

Together, they made canned soup and sandwiches. They sat on the kitchen floor, across from each other, and ate. Quinn told him some of the stuff that happened in her dream. She told him about how hot it was, and how it was the worst thing ever to be that hot, without any comfort whatsoever. With very few details, she told him about the part where he was shot, and how Michael told her nothing was set in stone.

Ajax agreed with the angel. "Everything'll be alright," he reminded her.

That night, they both went to bed exhausted. Quinn slept next to Ajax, with, of course, different quilts. The rest was much-needed, and they both knew deep down that a bad wind was blowing their way. It wouldn't be long until it reached its destination.

Chapter 28

Quinn spent most of her sleeping hours, with Michael, on a snow-covered mountain. It wasn't cold, like earth's winters, but it was just as beautiful. The only colors were white, green, and blue. Quinn was able to send herself to him during the dream. All she had to do was think of him before she fell asleep. Most of the time with him was just comfortable silence, or mind conversations. The only conversation they spoke aloud was what was in Quinn's heart.

"Michael, I fear what's to come. I don't want the pain that comes with the loss."

Michael smiled with understanding. "The pain of loss comes with being human. You're human; losing the ones we love hurts, but the pain won't last forever."

Quinn thought to herself for a moment.

"Michael, out of curiosity, what would our future've been like? Would I have met Ajax? I really wanna know what would've happened."

"Child, if that part was laid out, I'd give the information freely.   I'd like to think that you would have met a few years down the road, married and had beautiful babies, but Ajax's path wasn't laid in that direction," Michael said softly. "Being who I am, I wish I could help and save you from the pain you're to endure, and so does God," he added.

Quinn woke up, fully alert, and surprisingly well rested.   She heard the shower start; she jumped out of bed and dressed quickly.   "We're gonna make the most of the time we have worthwhile," she thought.   She wasn't going to tell Ajax where their path led.   Excited, she closed her eyes, and opened the bathroom door.

"Hurry up.   I wanna do something today: anything!"

She shut the door, and ran to the kitchen to make something quick for breakfast.   Quinn pulled out a couple of bowls and spoons, and then grabbed the cereal and milk.   She scarfed down her breakfast, and was making a pot of coffee, when Ajax entered the kitchen.

"Hey, look, the local peeping Tammy," Ajax chuckled.

"My eyes were closed," she said in complete innocence, shaking her head.

"Funny thing is, I actually believe you," Ajax replied, sitting at the table.

When the coffee was done, Quinn took the mugs to the table with her, and placed Ajax's in front of him.

"What's all the excitement about?" Ajax asked, finishing his last bite of cereal.

Quinn ran his bowl to the sink, and put the other stuff away.

"I dunno," she replied.

Quinn walked up, and put her arms around his neck.

"Is there anything you miss doing? Like something you used to do that you enjoy? Or maybe something you wanna knock off a bucket list?" she asked.

Ajax placed a hand on her arm, and pulled her around in front of him. He looked at her for a long moment, wondering where this was coming from. He stretched his leg out, and hooked her chair, bringing it right under her.

Quinn sat still, sweetly smiling at him.

"I don't have a bucket list. The things I used to like doing, or I thought I liked, would most likely anger, you and be viewed as sinful."

Quinn's smile faded.

"Why don't we just find new things that excite us?" Ajax said, bending down, and giving her a sweet kiss.

Quinn's smile returned.

"Fine, let's go see what's out there," Quinn said, jumping to refill their mugs.

"Wait, what was it that you did that was sinful?" she asked, concerned.

Ajax made an uncomfortable expression, took a deep breath, and opened his mouth to speak.

"No. No. No. Never mind, I don't wanna know," Quinn blurted out, after seeing the look that ran across his face.

"A conversation for another time," Ajax said, looking worried. He really hoped he hadn't ruined her good mood.

Quinn saw his face fall. She jumped on his lap, and kissed his cheek.

"What're we waiting for?" she asked.

Cruising down the highway, less than an hour from the cabin, they found a larger town on the map, called Cadenville. It looked to be a tourist town. Quinn sat, with the map laid out on her lap. At the moment, she wasn't really looking at it; her thoughts were elsewhere. Something weighed on her mind. She'd been thinking about it for a while, but kept dismissing it. She bit her lower lip.

"Dantanian knows where we are, and it won't be long before Ajax's father does, too. If my dreams are correct, there isn't much I can do," she thought.

"Hey, no long faces today. We're supposed to be having fun," Ajax said, putting his hand on her knee.

Quinn faked a smile.

"I'm just thinking about what kinda stuff we can find to do in Cadenville."

Ajax just gave her knee a squeeze, knowing she wasn't being truthful.

After two hours on the road, they arrived. The town was a busy place; the nice weather brought everyone in. They drove around the town, looking for something new. On the other side of town, there was an indoor and outdoor sportsplex. The sign read, "Wall Climbing Zip Lining and More!"

"Oh man, this looks so fun!" Ajax said, his voice rising with excitement.

Quinn smiled at his expression. His face lit up like the Fourth of July.

"Let's start on the inside, and work our way out," Ajax said, walking into the two-story building. On the inside, there was no second floor. About fifty feet from the door, there was a two-story wall. Ajax got them signed up, and they were assigned a guide. Quinn followed the men over to the wall. Her hands were sweaty, and she was starting to feel flushed. Ajax volunteered to go first. Quinn watched with amazement at how well he climbed. She almost screamed, when he lost his footing, and almost fell. Although someone was holding the rope below, she was still a little on edge.

When Ajax rappelled down, the sight made her insides turn.

"Your turn," Ajax said, holding the harness in his hand, as though it was a pair of underwear, and he was dressing a child. Quinn froze in place, where she had stood the whole time. Ajax handed the harness to the instructor, and walked over to her. Her eyes were still on the wall, and her breathing was deep.

Ajax held both of her hands, and bent down a little, for eye contact. "Hey, what's up?"

Quinn looked away from the wall, and focused on Ajax. "I ... I don't think I can do this," she said.

Ajax felt her hands start to shake.

"Hey, Babe, you don't have to do anything you don't wanna."

Quinn calmed down a bit, and shook her head.

"I think I should try," she said, licking her dry lips. "And could you hold the rope?" she added.

Ajax chuckled. "You have too much faith in me, but I will."

"It's not faith; it's trust," she corrected.

When Quinn had her harness on, she walked over to the wall, and took a deep breath.

"Hey, keep your eyes only on what you're doing. I'll advise you on the best places to put your feet, once you find the most comfortable place for your hands. Relax and have fun; that's why we came here."

Quinn nodded her head. The first three feet weren't too bad, but after that, the stones were farther apart. She paused for a minute, to regain the little bit of bravery she started with.

"Take your left foot, and place it on the yellow stone right under the blue one," Ajax called. "You're doing great; now push off with your left foot, and place your right foot on the black stone right above the green one," Ajax called again.

When Quinn reached up for the stone, her hand slipped, and she almost lost her footing. After grabbing hold again, she took a deep breath, calming her jitters.

"I'm good!"

After what seemed like forever, Quinn reached the top, and rang the bell, as she was told to do.

"Just fall now. I gotcha," Ajax yelled up.

Quinn looked down at him, asked herself whether he was crazy, and decided she should confirm her thoughts.

"Are you crazy?" she yelled back.

She could see Ajax trying really hard not to laugh.

"Would you like to climb down? It's harder, but I'll help guide you," Ajax yelled back up.

"Okay. Okay. Just fall?"

"Yeah, I have you. I'll bring you down as slow as I can," Ajax replied.

Quinn took a breath, closed her eyes, and let go. She fell, but not as fast as Ajax had. She opened her eyes when her feet touched the ground. Ajax was right there to greet her, and helped her out of the harness. There was no way he was going to let the instructor do it.

After they took a lunch break, they made their way outside to the zip line.

"This, I can't do," she said.

Before Ajax said anything, an instructor interrupted. "We have a couple's zip line harness, if you want to go together," she said, with a huge smile. "I really think the two of you will love it," she added, bouncing off the ground excitedly.

"Couple?" Ajax said, looking at Quinn.

Quinn blushed.

Ajax fell to one knee, and winked at the instructor. "Quinn, with you please couple zip line with me?"

Quinn rolled her eyes, and pushed his forehead, making him fall back onto the grass.

"If you promise, under any circumstance, you'll never, ever do that again," Quinn said, trying not to smile.

"Anything, for you," Ajax said, standing up, with a cocky smile on his face.

Two instructors harnessed them, and double and triple checked everything. They were extremely thorough; they even had a check list to go by. Ajax asked for Quinn to be in the back. She thought it almost looked like he was going to give her a piggyback ride.

"When we let go of the line, you can hang, or wrap your legs around," the male instructor advised.

"Oh, you guys're gonna love it," the woman added.

On the count of one … two … and on three, they let go. Quinn wrapped every limb around Ajax. Halfway through, she opened her eyes, and loosened her grip. The sight was stunning, as all the colors flashed by. She put her face closer to his.

"Wow, it's beautiful!"

Chapter 29

Ajax stopped to get milkshakes for the ride home. They couldn't decide what they wanted, so they got the three main flavors – chocolate, vanilla, and strawberry – and shared them. They talked about the excitement of their day, and laughed until they cried at some of the funny stuff that happened. A half-empty shake Quinn was working on malfunctioned, and the bottom of the cup came apart. The shake was all over her shirt.

"Oh, that's cold!" she shivered.

"My flannel shirt's in the back seat, if you wanna change into that." Ajax offered.

Quinn climbed into the back seat, took off the wet, sticky shirt, and replaced it with the flannel, which smelled just like Ajax. It was long enough to reach her thighs.

"Looks better on you," he winked.

Quinn smiled and blushed a bit.

"Did you have fun?" Quinn asked, climbing back into her seat in the front.

Ajax grabbed her hand, and held it.

"Yes. I enjoyed every moment. Even now is quite enjoyable."

Quinn gave his hand a squeeze; Ajax brought her hand to his lips, and kissed it.

"Today was pretty great," Quinn agreed. "I don't want it to end," she added, a little sadly.

"It doesn't have to; it's still early. Wanna go to Adam and Eve's?"

"Yeah. We missed dinner with them the other night," she said, remembering why.

They pulled up to Adam and Eve's a little after six in the evening. They knew the store would be closed, so they walked around back, and knocked.

After a minute or two, Eve opened the door.

"I had a feeling you guys would come over tonight. Just in time for dinner, too. Won't you stay and eat?"

Quinn smiled and gave Eve a hug, and whispered in her ear, "I knew you were there with me the other night. Thank you."

Eve squeezed her back. "Always, child."

They had dinner outside on the side deck. There wasn't enough room on the small dining table. They had steak, baked potatoes, corn on the cob, and individual bowls of tossed salad.

"Everything looks yummy," Ajax said, almost drooling.

Quinn giggled at him. He turned and winked at her, rubbing circles on her back.

"Come on, kids, sit," Adam demanded.

During dinner, Ajax told them everything they'd done. He was excited when he started

telling them about Quinn making it to the top of
the wall.

"I knew she could do it; I had no doubt," Ajax
explained.

While Ajax babbled, Eve caught Quinn's eye,
and winked at her, with a giddy smile.   All
throughout dinner, the guys talked about this and
that.   Every once in a while, Quinn and Eve
laughed at their excitement.   Everyone ate until
they could eat no more.

Ajax and Quinn volunteered to do the dishes.
Quinn washed and rinsed, and Ajax dried and put
the dishes away.   The kitchen was so small, they
couldn't help but be skin-to-skin close.   Ajax had
to reach over Quinn to put a serving plate away,
and his whole body pressed up against her.

"Sorry," he said.

"No, you aren't," Quinn said, laughing, and
she hip bumped him.

"You're right; I'm not sorry."

Ajax continued until the last dish was put
away.

Adam called in from the store front, and asked
Ajax for some help doing something.   As Ajax
passed behind Quinn, he pecked her on the cheek.

"Save me some coffee," he whispered.

Quinn giggled at him, and pushed him away
with her back end.   When she looked back at him,
he put his hands over his heart, pretending to fan
himself from the heat.   Quinn wrinkled her nose,
and smiled.

Eve and Quinn took their coffee to the deck,
and sat in the cool breeze.

"What's weighing on your mind, honey?" Eve asked. "And don't ya tell me I wouldn't understand; I understand more than you think," she added.

Quinn looked over at her, with a worried smile. "Someone's gonna be hurt, one way or another, and I'm just not ready for it."

Eve nodded her head. "There's pain in every path; I know this first hand."

Quinn looked at her with a shocked expression.

Eve smiled. "I know, 'cause only because I'm pure-hearted."

"Adam?" Quinn asked.

Eve shook her head. "He knows very little, but believes in all. Haven't ever had to tell him. Who knows: maybe he's like us, too, in some ways."

"What if you only had two paths: one that brings heartache, one that would save your heart from being broken?"

Eve smiled at her. "The path you choose will be the right one, no matter how it makes you feel."

Quinn looked at the ground, while sipping her coffee.

"All will fall where it may," Eve said, patting Quinn's arm.

Ajax looked out the deck door. "Quinn, we should be getting back. It's getting late."

Quinn nodded, and stood up to hug Eve; she hugged Adam on the way out. Ajax held her hand on the way to the car. The night air was cool, and the sun had been down a while. The crickets were out, loud and clear. When they reached the SUV, Ajax opened the door, but continued to hold her hand. Quinn looked at him. Ajax looked far away, but not unhappy. Quinn smiled, and leaned against the back door of the SUV, waiting for Ajax to return.

"Where did you go?" Quinn asked.

"Nowhere," Ajax replied, removing his hand from hers. "I know this day's to end, but, like you, I don't want it to."

Ajax raised both hands and held her blowing hair back. With free hands, she pulled him into a hug. After a long while, Ajax bent down, and kissed her softly.

"I had the perfect day," Quinn said, with her eyes still closed.

Ajax let out a breath of air he was holding.

"There'll be better days in our future," Ajax said, helping her into her seat.

Quinn knew that wasn't possible, but she wasn't going to spoil this for him.

Chapter 30

A week passed, and there were no incidents. Father David sent updates to Adam, and the last said there was no activity from Ajax's father. They doubted he had given up on the matter, but Quinn and Ajax were perfectly fine with the downtime. Everything and everyone from this realm, heaven, and hell was quiet. Quinn had not rested this well in weeks.

Quinn left Ajax asleep, and left him a note, saying she was heading to Adam's, to collect any messages that they received yesterday, when Adam traveled out of town. Quinn walked into the store, and the messages lay on the counter. One was from her mom, one from Father David, and one with no writing on the outside. She opened the one from her mom, and began reading:

Dear Quinn,
Ajax's mom and I are leaving for a singles'
cruise that Father David booked for us. That

*man is all drama now-a-days. I'm just joking,
darling. He said something along the line that
someone at church had won the tickets, and
couldn't make it, due to other obligations. We
should only be gone three weeks all together.
That includes all the stopping on the islands,
and the drive home when we dock. I left the
fridge stocked, just in case you come home
early. When I get back, maybe we can expand
the garden, like I wanted to last year. I can't
wait to talk to you, baby. I'll call at the first
dock we get to. I love you.*

Mom.

Quinn chuckled to herself. "Father David is
really trying to keep them busy. A single cruise,
really?" she thought.

Quinn set her mother's letter on the top of the
pile, and picked them all up; the blank one fell to
the floor, opening up. Quinn bent to pick it up;
the writing was neat and polished.

Dear Ajax,

*You did the right thing contacting your
father. I think he'll forgive you, if we
marry and you set down your roots, like
your father did. The family business needs
a new face, and we'd run everything, with
the help of your father. Come home; we
miss you. I'm sure we can make this work
between us. Don't you miss what we had?
I sure do.*

Katie

Quinn didn't even bother closing the door when she ran out, jumped in the SUV, and sped off, squealing the tires, out of the small parking lot. Quinn was painfully angry. Her pulse was throbbing in her temples.

When she got to her turn off, she didn't even bother slowing down. She took the turn going way too fast, but made it successfully. The long, first road seemed longer than normal. She was inches from the porch when she braked hard, barely stopping. After shutting off the SUV, she jumped out, and ran into the house.

Ajax sat at the kitchen table, smiling when she entered the cabin. His smile faded, when he saw the look on her face.

"What's wrong?" Ajax asked, standing up.

Quinn was a raging mess; she had trouble talking, so she threw the papers at him. Ajax picked up the open one, and bowed his head in shame.

"You're a fool! You think you'll actually be forgiven? You think that you'll marry and have a happily ever after?" Quinn asked in a low, but angry, voice.

"Katie's no one to me," Ajax replied.

"You're quite the fool, aren't you?" Quinn asked, out of breath. "I don't care who Katie is to you. I would have no issue with it. Being together was great, just a perk. I'd give it all up, if I knew you were safe."

Ajax's face tightened, and he looked a little hurt. He tossed the letter on the table.

"I only did this to keep you safe," Ajax said loudly.

"You don't get it. Everything that's happened is because your father and Hell want you dead," Quinn said through gritted teeth. "Doesn't matter what your father says, it's not his choice now," she added.

Quinn turned, and made her way down the hall full speed, with Ajax on her heels. She started pulling thing from drawers, and throwing them into the duffle bags.

"Stop!" Ajax said, his voice raised.

Quinn spun around. "You have no idea what you've done. There's a good chance they know where we are," Quinn said, shoving past him, heading to the bathroom.

"Come on, calm down, Quinn. They don't. Maybe this just stalled them," Ajax said. "This could be why they've slowed down, waiting for my response," he added.

Quinn stilled herself, with her back to Ajax. If only she could tell him everything. "It wouldn't change anything. Everything'll still happen as planned, as I've been shown," she thought miserably.

Quinn turned around with a single tear running down her face. "I wanna go home. Anything that they plan can happen here or there. I just wanna be home when it does happen." Quinn was so upset that her stomach and chest hurt. She sobbed from the emotional pain. "I just wanna go home."

Ajax had seen Quinn in pain more than once, but this pain was so much worse to watch. She was doubled over, sobbing. He just stood there, not knowing what to do.

After a few moments, Ajax sat on the floor in front of her. He lifted her head. "Okay, let's go home."

By nightfall, the car was packed up. Quinn grabbed the notebook from the book shelf, and shoved it into her bag. The ride was quiet, and dreadfully long, but this time they took the highway, and made it home within a few hours. When Ajax pulled up to her house, it was dark. Father David was sitting on the porch, waiting. Quinn grabbed her stuff, but dropped it at her feet as she hugged Father David.

"I realize you're angry about us leaving. I'm sorry for that. I know for a fact if something bad's gonna happen – and it will – I wanna be home. 'Cause there's no stopping this; hiding isn't gonna fix this path we're on," she whispered in his ear.

Quinn grabbed her stuff again, and walked into her dark house. She opened the door to her bedroom, dropped everything, fell on her bed, and cried herself to sleep.

Quinn opened her eyes to light shining in the bedroom window. Her eyes were sore from crying. She turned around, and Ajax was sitting in the chair never to her bed, just staring at her. Quinn couldn't read his expression; his face was void. They stared at each other for the longest time, until Ajax spoke.

"Katie, and any other part of my past, is always gonna just up and bite me in the ass." Ajax paused, and swallowed hard. "I'm not sure if I've already lost you, or I'm gonna lose you slowly, when you learn everything about me."

Quinn sat up, and folded her knees up to her chin, facing Ajax.

"Loss hurts, and you'll lose me someday. It won't be willingly, though."

Ajax's face softened a little.

"I learned everything thing I need to know about you. As for your past, God's forgiven you; now you must forgive yourself."

Ajax still looked as though sadness was dragging him to his grave. He knelt down beside her bed, grabbed her legs, and pulled her to him. "I have this bad feeling we're gonna be torn apart indefinitely."

Quinn hugged his head to her chest. "Everything'll be okay," she lied, with a tear escaping her eye.

Chapter 31

Quinn opened the doors to her hometown church, and a rush of peace ran through her. She pulled a delicate, white chapel veil out of her handbag and placed it over her hair. Quinn wore a light pink, flowy, Empire dress , which fell past her knees; the sleeves were see-through, and wide, for comfort.

"Bless me, Father, for I have sinned.   I purposely lied to someone I love, and I've lied to him multiple times. The worst part is, I can't tell him the truth. I'm sure there's a multitude of sins I've commented since my last confession, but this one's really weighing on my soul. Even if I didn't lie, I wouldn't be able to tell the truth.   Not without committing a different kind of sin."

After confession, Quinn walked to the coffee shop across the street, ordered a cup of coffee, and sat down. She dug through her purse, and located her phone. She dialed Adam and Eve's number, and listen to it ring six times before Eve's soft voice came on the line.

"Hello?"

"Hi, Eve. It's.."

"Oh, dear, I know who this is," Eve chuckled.

Quinn smiled to herself, and remembered why she'd called.

"Eve, we're no longer at the cabin, and I'm so sorry we didn't tell you when we left. We left kinda in a rush."

"Yes. Father contacted us when you arrived home."

"Eve, uh, can I ask you something?"

"Sure ya can, dear."

Quinn gave Eve the run down from picking up the letter and how she handled herself.

"Quinn, although we have a gift, we're still human. The way you reacted was exactly what I've done myself. Make amends, and apologize for only what you're sorry for."

The line was silent for a moment before Quinn spoke.

"Would it make me a bad person for only saying sorry for raising my voice, but not for using the words I did?"

Eve and Quinn laughed light-heartedly.

"Only apologize for what you're sorry for, nothing more," Eve said once again.

Quinn chatted with Eve for another 20 minutes, before saying their goodbyes. Before leaving the coffee shop, she ordered a few different bagels, with cream cheese on the side, a dozen assorted donuts, and two coffees to go. Food always helped in stressful times.

Quinn arrived home with a pep in her step, and she took everything to the kitchen. To her surprise, there was already a spread of food on the kitchen table. Quinn raised an eyebrow, and set the bags and coffee on the counter. She looked at the table again. There were scrambled eggs, toast, orange juice, bacon, and fried taters.

"Moms not home," she thought.

The taters and eggs were browned pretty well, so Ajax must have cooked.

Quinn walked to the end of the hall.

"Ajax?" she yelled.

She didn't want to walk in on him changing, or something.

"Ajax," she yelled again, walking down the hall, looking into the rooms, before she walked into her own. Nothing. No one was there. Ajax wasn't there.

"Where'd he get off to," she thought

She stood there for a moment, with her hands on her hips, and started to worry. She jumped when the front door slammed shut.

"Quinn? You home?" Ajax's voice was loud enough to hear throughout the house.

"Yeah, I'm here," she said, making her way down the hall.

Ajax looked relieved. "Where were you?" he asked. "I just got back from looking all over town."

"Well, you missed two places: the church and the coffee shop."

Ajax looked a little annoyed. "Ya, I guess I did," he said, making his way to the kitchen, his shoulders tight and jagged.

"There's food, probably cold now," he added, with annoyance slithering off him, enough to make the floors slippery.

Quinn caught up to Ajax, and grabbed his arm, turning him. His eyes looked hurt, but his face was hard.

"What?" he said in an angered whisper.

After a few long moments, his face was the same as it started; Quinn spoke.

"I'm sorry for yelling at you at the cabin. I'm sorry about leaving and not letting you know, and I'm extremely sorry about being sarcastic."

Ajax's demeanor softened a little, but his face stayed the same. He rubbed the top of his head roughly, and let out a deep breath.

"No, it's fine; let's just eat."

Quinn quickly closed the small distance and put her arms around his waist. At first, he was still breathing deeply, and his body was hard and still, his arms still at his sides. After a minute, his body sort of melted, like butter, and his large arms wrapped around her head. Ajax gave her a kiss on the top of her head. Quinn didn't want to let go, unsure whether his face would still be the same.

"I'm so, so sorry," Quinn said, peeking up at him.

"I am, too," Ajax said, still not smiling, but not cold, as he was before.

"Let's eat," Ajax added, removing himself from her, and heading to the kitchen.

Quinn realized nothing that she just said or did had helped him at all. He was just pretending, to stop her attempts at making him feel better.

As the day ended, and the next day came and went, Ajax was still a little chilly and distant. Quinn gave him the space and time he needed to work through whatever it was that caused the strain between them. Quinn took herself back to work, to make the days more bearable, and to build up her bank account. With her mom gone, the only person she had to talk to, besides Father David, was Ajax, and he hadn't said more than a handful of words to her in days. It bothered Quinn, for a little while, but she hoped it'd clear up soon. At first, she wished she'd never fought to leave the cabin; everything'd still be okay. Deep down, she realized she took this path for a reason, even though it hurt at the moment.

Chapter 32

Ajax lay in his own bed, with a damp towel wrapped around his waist. Quinn was already off to work. He had stayed until she left, and then had gone to his mom's house. He felt like things were falling apart, and he'd just been in a bad mood since the other afternoon, when he and Quinn griped at each other. Even though they apologized to each other, he still couldn't shake the mood he was in. He stayed clear of Quinn as much as he could. He wasn't mad at her, but didn't want to snap at her, and start an argument. He could tell his distance bothered her a little, but she seemed to be coping, and going about her day.

At times, he wished they never left the cabin. Since they'd been home, nothing has been the same. The fun was over, and he didn't see it returning. He missed Quinn, even though she was always there. He knew he only felt like this because of how he was acting. Nothing about Quinn had changed. Ajax was still a little upset at himself for sending a letter to his father, and maybe a little hurt about Quinn calling him out on his foolishness. No one but his dad had ever talked to him like that. The ladies he dated would never have talked to him like that. He knew that was only because they wanted something from him. Quinn had nothing to lose by telling him off.

Ajax crawled out of bed, tossed his towel in the hamper, and dressed. He put on a pair of dark blue jeans and a red short-sleeved, button-down. He was going to church, to see whether Father David was free to grab a cup of coffee. When he pulled up to the church, Father David was outside, pulling weeds from the flower bed, and talking it up with some older ladies, who were helping him. Instead of disturbing their conversation, he headed across the street to the coffee shop, where he order a cup, and sat down.

Ajax was lost in a book he was reading on his phone when his table jolted. He looked up, and sitting across from him was Katie. He wasn't surprised to see her, even though he didn't expect it would be this soon. He looked her over a few times. He could see how she'd gotten to him in the past. She was drop-dead gorgeous. She had long, straight, blonde hair, and striking, blue eyes, which people noticed before anything else. She was tall, maybe a couple of inches shorter than Ajax. Ajax was never a leg man, but her legs went on for miles.

"Katie, to what do I owe the pleasure?" Ajax asked, looking her over once more.

She smiled her perfect teeth at him, and placed her hand over his on the table. "Ajax, you're so silly. I want you to come home. I miss you," she said, pouting with her full, kissable lips.

Ajax sat back to remove his hand from under hers. "I don't want that life; I never did," Ajax replied.

"You don't have to want it. Doesn't it make it better, if I come with the package?" she said, winking.

"Listen, Katie," he said, standing up. "You're beautiful, and that was the only thing I was into then," he said, as he walked out the door. When he got to his car, Katie put herself in front of him, pulled him close, and kissed him, open-mouthed and all.

Ajax was stunned for a moment, but then he jerked away. "What's wrong with you?" Ajax said through gritted teeth.

Now Katie wasn't smiling. "I won't tell your dad where you are, yet. I want you to come home on your own, not in a body bag," Katie said, pouting yet again; she looked a little angry.

"A body bag is the only way they'll get me back there," Ajax shot back.

Katie said no more; she moved away from his car, and headed down the sidewalk in long strides. Ajax took a minute to steady his breathing, and he looked around at his surroundings.

Father David was no longer outside, gardening, and the streets were kind of empty. The only person he saw was a girl in torn jeans, a white tank top, stained with grease, and her curly hair pulled into a messy, distraught bun; it was Quinn. He watched her walk, and realized he didn't know what he ever saw in Katie. Katie was pretty, yes, but Quinn was perfect. The mood he'd been in was completely gone.

Ajax paused.

"Oh, no, she's seen everything," he thought, although the way Quinn was walking didn't seem mean.

Ajax looked down at his phone. He noticed Quinn was getting out of work a few hours late. She pulled 13 hours today.

Ajax hopped in the car, and made it back to her house as the front door closed. He parked in his mom's driveway, and walked over to Quinn's. He didn't bother knocking; he just walked in. He didn't notice any movement in the kitchen, so he walked down the hall to her room; the door was wide open. Her back was to him, as she collected clothing from her dresser. When she looked up, she saw him standing there in the doorway.

Ajax didn't give her time to say anything before he spoke. "You didn't see what you thought you saw."

"No worries, Ajax, I didn't see anything that'll ruin me." Quinn said this, and made it seem believable.

"Quinn, your eyes say something very different."

Quinn turned, and looked in the mirror.

"My eyes look very tired," she said, looking at him through the mirror.

Ajax walked up to her. Quinn didn't shy away, or run off. Ajax stopped just an inch from touching her. He noticed a bead of sweat making its way down the back of her neck.

"That was Katie."

Quinn looked down, avoiding eye contact.

"She kissed me. I stopped her. That was that."

Quinn popped her neck by moving it side-to-side. Her body ached from all the walking, pulling, and lifting she'd done today.

"Okay," she said, making eye contact through the mirror.

"Okay? Like, okay, you're too mad to talk?"

"No. It means I believe you," Quinn replied. "You've never given me any real reason not to trust you," she added.

Ajax turned Quinn around. She wasn't mad, and she didn't seem upset. At that moment, Ajax wanted nothing more than to kiss her. Quinn saw his look, too.

"Ajax, please, I just really, really wanna get a shower, please."

Ajax went back to her room 15 minutes later, with a glass of water, and leftovers from the fridge. Quinn was already out of the shower, but was passed out on her bed, with just her after-shower robe on. Her face was expressionless, and she was out cold. Ajax grabbed the quilt from the back of the chair, and covered her up. He went to shut off the bathroom light. The bathroom was a mess; Quinn always cleaned up after a shower. The only thing she'd managed to do was get her dirty clothes into the basket. He picked up the towel, and hung it on the back of the door. He cleaned up the sink, and put away over-the-counter painkillers she must have taken.

When the bathroom was picked up, Ajax plopped down in the chair next to the bed. It'd dawned on him that she'd been working these hours for four days, trying to keep away from him and his bad mood. Ajax rubbed his face in frustration.

"Lord, please forgive me and my stupid ways," he whispered.

Chapter 33

Quinn woke up in a dream state, which she'd never entered before. A soft and strong hand was tracing up and down her arm. It gave her goosebumps, and she smiled and shivered. The hand lightly slid up her arm, and brushed her hair from her neck; the lips that belonged to the hand lightly began kissing her neck, and breathing warm, fresh breath on her skin. Quinn turned to see who had her interest. When she saw the face, she didn't recognize it, but she wasn't at all scared. The black-eyed, dark-haired man smiled calmly at her, tracing her cheekbone with his thumb.

"Good morning, my darling wife," he said, still smiling beautifully.

"Hi," she whispered.

His skin was flawless, and so warm to the touch. Quinn smiled back slightly.

"It's alright, my sweet darling wife; you were dreaming."

Quinn nodded, a little confused.

"Yeah, I...," Quinn said in a soft exhale.

Dantanian moved closer, closing what little gap was between them. He leaned in closer, but Quinn didn't budge. He smiled at her, seeming to be relieved, and then put his mouth on hers. His kiss was so soft and sweet that Quinn's mind forgot all about the confusion.

"Dantanian is the name of my husband," she thought, smiling. Everything she knew was just a bad dream, from which she was finally awake.

His kiss grew more heated and encouraging. He lightly pressed her mouth open for a deeper kiss, and she relaxed and openly received it. Quinn's breath became heavy, and her heart started to race, but she noticed Dantanian's actions were the same as they started. When she started to wonder, he kissed harder, or grabbed her tighter, and every thought she had melted away and was forgotten.

After a while of steamy kisses, he removed the covers from their bodies. Quinn looked down at herself. She was clothed in a very short, forest green, silk nighty.

"Ew, why would I pick out something so ugly?" she cringed.

Before she could think any more, he moved his body over hers, and again she was lost in his eyes. His body slithered softly onto hers, and she barely registered the weight of his body on hers. He proceeded to kiss her chin, neck, and collar bone, and worked his way around the ugly nighty. Quinn felt the warmth of his breath with every kiss on her body. As he descended to her lower abdomen, the heat from his breath became a little too warm, and the more excited he got, the more scorching his mouth and breath became. Quinn let out a cry when her hip and thigh felt as though they were doused in fire. She looked down, and the ugly gown had burn holes, with seared skin underneath. Quinn started to panic, as reality came flooding back, along with the pain. "Nothing here is real, except for the pain."

Now that he had lost her to reality, his sweetness disappeared. He looked just as evil as she remembered. He climbed back up her body, smiling, and the weight of him was much heavier than before. His mouth moved over her neck and chest. Quinn bucked and screamed in pain.

"Get off! Get off!" She screamed in anger.

He laughed into her searing skin.

Quinn began to see red.

Suddenly, she felt his arms try to circle around her. His arms were strong. In her ears, she heard someone calling her name in panic.

"Quinn, get up! Wake up!"

Quinn's eyes flew open, and the arms that were holding her were now kicked to the floor. Quinn sat up, her eyes wild. She looked at Ajax, sitting on the floor, with his hand held up in surrender. Quinn looked down at herself. Her robe was pretty much burned off, and the white tank top and matching white, cotton underwear had burn marks, the same as the ugly nighty had a moment before. Quinn went feral. She scrambled out of bed, and into her bathroom, sliding and slipping as she tried to shut the door. She looked in the mirror on the back of her door. Her body had mouth-shaped burn marks in places she would never allow. Her face looked scary and wild. Her body was hunched over, like a football play ready to attack.

She jumped backwards, into the shower, when the door flew open. Ajax stood frozen, his eyes wide with horror. Quinn took his expression as disgust, as she would have herself.

"Get out!" she half screamed, her voice very hoarse. "Don't look at me; get the hell out of here."

Ajax held his hands up, as if he was talking down a mad person.

"Quinn, you're shaking, and we need to treat the burns."

Quinn shook her head wildly. "No. No, you're not touching me," she said, her voice still raised. Her eyes started tearing up, not from pain but fear and anger. "I'm not sure if this is real," she whispered, more to herself.

Ajax thought for a moment, his face soft and gentle. "This is real; what happened to you was in a dream, or something," he said softly. "I won't hurt you, never." Ajax said, as he made the sign of the cross and began to pray. "Christ, be with us: Christ within us, Christ behind us, Christ before us, Christ beside us, Christ to win us, Christ to comfort and restore us. Christ beneath us, Christ above us, Christ in quiet, Christ in danger, Christ in hearts of all that love us, Christ in mouth of friend and stranger. I bind unto myself the Name, the strong Name of the Trinity; by invocation of the same. The Three in One, and One in Three, of Whom all nature hath creation, eternal Father, Spirit, Word: praise to the Lord of my salvation, salvation is of Christ the Lord. Amen."

Suddenly, out of nowhere, the room fell quiet. Quinn still looked freaked out, but a calmness was coming over her, and her body started to relax. A look of shame came across her face. The prayer helped her open her mind, to see the real truth.

"I don't want you to see me like this. I can't stand myself right now," Quinn whispered, holding back a sob stuck in her throat. "I ... I, uh, I just need to shower," she added, her lower lip quivering.

Ajax took a breath. He stepped in, took a towel off the shelf, and put in around her. "I'll find you something to put on," he said, walking out of the bathroom shutting the door.

"Please leave it open some," Quinn said quickly.

Ajax left the door ajar as he headed to find clothing, after he heard the shower start.

Quinn started the shower fully clothed, and let the water become completely hot. When she could no longer take the stinging on her skin, she turned the cold water on just enough to keep the pain at bay. She quickly removed the remaining clothing. Some clothing stuck painfully to her burned skin. Quinn scrubbed her body raw, even the burns themselves. As painful as it was, she needed to make sure she was clean, and even scrubbing wasn't helping all that much.

Quinn finished showering, and wrapped herself in a large towel. On the sink, she found a clean jogging suit. While she dressed, she let her mind go numb, so she wouldn't have to rethink what had happened. When she headed out of the bathroom, the sun was already up, and, to her relief, her bedroom was empty. The numbing started to fade, and her panic grew. She walked over to her bed, and striped all her bedding. She didn't plan to keep it, with the scorch marks. She gathered it all in her arms, and made her way down the hall, through the kitchen, and out the back door, where she tossed it all in the large, empty trash bin.

Ajax was leaning on the fridge when she entered the house, and he handed her a very large mug of coffee, with cream and sugar. "Why don't we stay at my mom's tonight? I know it won't make a difference, but maybe you could actually be safe, and rest," Ajax offered.

"Alright," Quinn agreed, walking away, and sitting at the kitchen table.

"That was easy," Ajax thought, joining her at the table.

Ajax wanted so badly to ask her about what happened in her dream, but, at the same time, he really didn't want to know. From how she reacted, it had to be worse than the last time, and he knew the last time was really bad. Ajax was more worried about her not knowing whether he was really himself. This was the first time she couldn't tell the difference between here and wherever she went in her dreams.

Chapter 34

After filling an overnight bag with only things she needed for the night, Quinn and Ajax headed over to Ajax's house. Ajax unlocked the door, and held it open for her. Quinn slowly walked in, realizing she hadn't been in this house since she'd been a baby. She walked right into an entry hall: a short hallway, with creamed-coffee walls, and mirrors on either side. To the right sat a shoe rack, and to the left, a line of coat hooks; under that was a bench, with a thick, leather seat, to sit while removing outside wear. Ajax took her bag, and slung it over his shoulder.

"Come on," he said, jerking his head in the direction he wanted to go. When he entered the next room, he hit the light switch. The room was open, and expanded from the living room, where they stood, all the way to the kitchen. The color seemed the same as the entry hall, but a little darker brown. With the bright lighting they had, it wasn't dark, despite the color of the walls. All the furniture was dark, with red and white pillows and throws lying on the couches and chairs. On the coffee table sat a rectangular vase, which started from one side of the coffee table, and ended on the other end. It was filled with water marbles, water, and real, red and white roses. In the living room, there wasn't a television, just a fireplace built out of a bookcase, which still held a large number of books. The wall color flowed into the dining room, as well, with the same style. The kitchen, on the other hand, was completely different. Everything had a sterile look: white and stainless steel.

"This is my dad's doing, when they were together. Not exactly my mom's style, but cost way too much to change," Ajax said, answering her unasked question.

"Come on," Ajax said walking to the left side of the house. There was another hall.

"This was our guest room, if you wanna stay in here."

Quinn nodded her head, and Ajax placed her backpack right inside the door. Quinn peeked inside. There weren't any closets in this room, and only one window. The room was pale blue, with a double bed covered in a red floral quilt, and a standard, white nightstands on either side.

Ajax grabbed her hand.

"Here's the main bath," Ajax pointed as he walked past the bathroom. At the end of the hall was a door, which opened up to a set of stars, descending into a basement. Once they reached the bottom of the stairs, it didn't look like a typical basement. On one side, there was a small gym area. The equipment seemed to be on the older side.

"This used to be where my dad hid when I was little. Mom converted it into a place of my own, after he left."

Ajax walked past the mini gym, turned left, and she followed. They walked right into Ajax's room. It even had his scent. On the far wall rested a king bed, which was covered in a black comforter and piles of pillows. On the wall opposite, there was a large television. At the end of his bed, he had a loveseat, with a red throw blanket. On the right wall, there was a closet on wheels.

"My room must be pretty bland," Quinn joked.

"Nah, I like it," Ajax replied, walking to his closet and taking out a grey pullover. He removed the shirt he was wearing, and replaced it with the other.

"I'm hungry. How about you?" Ajax asked, walking back to her.

"A little, I guess," she answered.

"Order in, or go out?" he asked.

"Order in," she responded.

Ajax was relieved that she picked order in; they could just relax and enjoy movies.

After a few moments discussion, they decided on a meat lover's pizza and a spinach, mushroom, and chicken pizza. Ajax made iced tea while they waited for the pizza to arrive. Quinn sat at the bar, and observed. Ajax could sense her eyes on him, so he thought he'd break the silence.

"So, when the pizza comes, wanna eat and put a movie in?"

Quinn nodded, and opened her mouth to speak, when the doorbell rang, making her jump up out of the bar seat. Ajax quickly moved to her, and patted her shoulder.

"Just the pizza," Ajax reassured her.

They ate their pizza, and watched a couple of movies, sitting on the floor in Ajax's room. He had the softest carpet ever, and so thick. Quinn sat and kind of followed what was going on, as did Ajax. When the movie ended, they packed up the boxes and cups, to put everything away before going to bed.

"I just locked up. I think I'm gonna call it a night," Ajax announced.

Ajax walked Quinn to the guest bedroom, opened the door, and turned on the light.

"You good?" he asked, moving aside, so she could go in.

Quinn nodded. "Good night."

Ajax bade her good night, and continued on his way.

Quinn pulled a night shirt out of her bag, and changed. She hit the light switch, and crawled under the quilt for warmth. This room seemed to be colder than the rest of the house, possibly because the door had been closed.

Quinn lay there for a couple of hours, trying to fall asleep. She wasn't having much luck. She was scared that, if she did, the dream would repeat itself. Now, thinking about it, she'd just scared herself some more. Quinn grabbed her phone from the nightstand, and used it as a light. She tiptoed out of the guest room, to the end of the hall, and down the stars. When she opened the door, it squealed as she walked in. Ajax rolled over, and sat up.

"Hey, you alright?"

Quinn was embarrassed. "Kinda scared," she whispered, trying not to get upset.

Ajax pulled back the comforter on the other side of him, and patted the bed. Quinn made her way to the bed with the light of her phone. She set the phone down, and crawled into the bed. Ajax met Quinn in the middle, and lay down, with his arm behind her. Quinn lay back, and then curled herself on her side, with her head on his bare chest. Quinn could hear the rhythm of his heartbeat, and it was comforting. He closed his arm around her, and she was no longer scared.

"Thank you," Quinn whispered in the darkness.

"Any time; there isn't any way you'd hear a guy complain about this," he joked. His chest shook in silent laughter. Quinn got his joke, and poked his side. After that, no one said a word. They fell asleep together, and slept all night without incident.

Quinn opened her eyes to a little light streaming through the tiny window, close to the ceiling. The room was still darkened, but she could see everything. She never moved from the position she fell asleep in. She looked up at Ajax. She didn't want to move too much, and wake him.

"Checking me out?" he said in a gruff, morning voice.

"A little," she admitted.

Ajax smiled, and closed his eyes again.

"Nice to know you still like me a little."

Quinn sat up on her elbow, her hair falling over half her face onto Ajax. She suddenly had the urge to tell him everything from her dream. Well, almost everything.

"He got inside my head," she said.

Ajax opened his mouth to say something, but Quinn shushed him. She knew that if she didn't tell him now, she never would.

"I woke up with my back to him. When I turned around, I wasn't scared. It was weird. The way I was feeling didn't make sense at all, because the face didn't match the vision of the person in my head. What I was feeling was how I do about you. That's why I allowed him to do everything he was doing. If it hadn't started burning, I wouldn't have stopped him. Why would I? In my mind, he made me believe we were married, and everything else that had been happening was the dream."

Quinn wiped angry tears from her face. Then she continued. "I enjoyed every moment, until the pain started. I felt disgusting and unclean. I just can't seem to make it go away. If it was a normal dream, fine, but it wasn't. His touch was so real. The way I felt, I know is real, but he used the way I feel for you, and made it connect to him. I'm not sure why I couldn't fight him, like I have been for the longest time. Maybe he's getting stronger, or I'm getting weaker."

Ajax lay there, tight-jawed, trying to hide the anger that was roaring to come alive.

"So the burn marks were everywhere he was?" Ajax asked bluntly.

Quinn didn't answer, and looked away. That was Ajax's answer. Ajax calmed his anger, when he noticed that Quinn might think he was disgusted by her, too. Ajax pulled her down, and rolled over to look her in the eyes.

"I'm real. This is real," he said, putting his fingers through hers. "The dream may have been real, but not as real as this." Ajax laid his head down facing her profile. Quinn could feel his warm breath on her face.

"I know; I just.... The gross part is that I enjoyed it," Quinn said, suddenly sick. She placed her hand on her stomach, with a nasty taste in the back of her mouth.

"Quinn, there's nothing to feel guilty about. What you felt was normal. I'm just happy you feel that way about me," Ajax said, smiling.

"Well, thanks," Quinn said, glowing red. "Not sure that makes it any better," she added.

Ajax covered her hand with his, and gave her a small kiss on the cheek.

"You like me. You want me," Ajax chanted in her ear, teasingly.

Quinn looked over at him. He smiled, quite pleased with himself.

"Stop it," she said, embarrassed.

Ajax stopped smiling.

"I know what'll make you feel better," Ajax said, turning her chin, so she looked at him. "I feel the same exact way about you. Lucky I've built up a little self-control, being around you all the time."

Ajax bent down, and kissed her softly on the lips.

"It's easy having self-control with me. I don't have a low self-esteem, but after seeing Katie, I can understand the lack of control," Quinn said in a normal, conversation tone.

Ajax chuckled a little at how nonchalantly she said it.

"No, it had nothing to do with self-control. Girls like that have little to no self-esteem, or respect for themselves, and I used it to my advantage. Like a lot of guys do. Something I'm not proud of. Here's an example: remember we had apple pie on your porch, our first time really hanging out?"

Quinn nodded.

"Well, anyone else, I would've put a move on."

Quinn looked a little annoyed. "What's wrong with me?" she asked.

"I really didn't wanna be kicked down under," Ajax responded, chuckling. "Plus, I started falling for you, the day I almost toppled you and your mother over."

"Really? Why?" Quinn asked.

"I dunno; you just had a white glow around you, and you're beautiful," Ajax answered her question.

"A white glow?" Quinn asked, laughing a little in surprise. "You had the same glow, and you still do. I see it all the time, like it's meant to be there," Quinn said.

"Yeah, it's the same for me," Ajax said. I guess we can be crazy together," he added.

Chapter 35

Ajax accompanied Quinn to Saturday evening Mass. With her arm in his, he guided her through the chatty crowd. When they reached the steps of the church, Ajax released her arm, so she could remove her chapel veil.

"Can I buy you a cup of coffee, pretty lady?" Ajax asked, nonchalantly hanging his arm over her shoulder.

"Uh huh," Quinn responded enthusiastically, smiling up at him.

As they slowly walked across the street to the coffee shop, Ajax asked, "So, whatcha think about the Mass?"

"Beautiful, as ever," she replied.

Walking into the coffee shop, he dropped his arm, and took hold of her hand. The place smelled of coffee, vanilla, and cinnamon. They reached the counter, and Ajax ordered two large coffees and two massive cinnamon buns. Through the glass case, Quinn could tell they were fresh out of the oven. The white frosting was thin, and dripping from the sides as the server put them on dinner-sized plates.   Quinn looked up at Ajax, raising one brow.

Ajax chuckled.   "What you don't eat, I will," he said, after pressing his lips to her forehead. "When I first got to town, Mom bought me one, and I'm hooked," he added.

"Never had them before; I guess I was missing out, huh?" Quinn voiced.

After receiving their coffee and buns, they found a little love seat, empty in an unoccupied corner of the café, where they made themselves comfortable.   Ajax laughed, as Quinn cut up her bun like a pizza.   Quinn took some white frosting, and put it on his nose for laughing, which made him laugh even harder.

"Here, I stop laughing, if you take a real bite out of mine," he offered.

Quinn took a bite, and knew right away why she wanted to cut hers.   She had frosting all over her lips and cheeks.

"There," she said, grabbing a napkin, wiping her cheeks off, and licking her lips.

Ajax dipped his head, and closed his lips on her upper lip.

"Missed a spot."

Quinn shook her head.

Ajax gave her a quick peck on the lips.

"What? I couldn't let it go to waste."

Quinn couldn't resist his sweetness, and gave him a lingering kiss, which left him wanting more.

"I'm not one to waste a good moment," she smiled.

"So, this is why you won't come home, huh?"

Quinn and Ajax looked up, and Ajax cleared his throat. Katie stood only a few feet away. She was wearing a short, tight, black skirt, and an even tighter, apple-red shirt, which fell off her shoulders. Her long, straight, beautiful, blonde hair was tied up in a tight ponytail, on top of her head, making her neck and bare shoulders even more enticing. She was sporting high-heeled boots, which made her long legs seem to go on forever.

Quinn glanced at Ajax. Katie's looks seemed to have no effect on him, which was impressive, because, for Quinn, Katie's looks were quite intimidating.

"I thought you were leaving?" Ajax spat.

Katie put her hands on her hips. "I can't go home empty handed."

Quinn felt a meltdown coming on.

"Take a cinnamon bun with you," Ajax responded, with no amusement on his face.

"Come on, Ajax, Daddy's gonna be upset with me. He already threatened to marry me off to Buddy," she whined.

Quinn was starting to understand why her looks weren't working. Her personality was horrible. If it wasn't so bad, she'd have a hard time holding back from laughing.

Quinn put her hand on Ajax's shoulder. "I'll meet you outside."

Ajax put his hand on her upper thigh, and squeezed. "No, let's just go home."

When Ajax and Quinn stood to leave, Katie stepped in front of them. Now, Quinn was getting a little irritated. She looked at Ajax, and smiled.

"I thought you don't like to waste? Would you please take those up there, and asked them to box them?"

Ajax waited a moment, wanting to argue. "Fine," he said, grabbing the plates, and taking them up to the counter.

"You know he's not into you, right?" Katie said smugly.

Quinn gave her best smile. "Katie, I know what you're trying to do. Believe it or not, I attended school with people like you. Your words have no effect on me. If Ajax wanted to go home, he could. It's called free will, and, trust me when I say this, I'm not stopping him from leaving."

Katie opened her mouth to say something, but Quinn cut her off with a stern look.

"Stop with the whining. I can't do anything, with you approaching us in town, but you come to our homes, and I'll show you another use for those very ugly boots." Quinn smiled a very fake smile. "Enjoy your stay."

Quinn walked away, leaving Katie with her open mouth and red face. Ajax caught a glimpse, as he caught up with Quinn.

"What'd ya say to her?"

Quinn just raised her shoulders. "I just told her to enjoy her stay," Quinn answered, taking her paper cup from his hand.

"Uh huh," Ajax countered.

Before he could ask her again, Father David was yelling, and waving them down. When he reached them, he was a little winded.

"Hey, I need a favor from both of you."

Quinn and Ajax looked at one another.

"What's up, Father?" Ajax smiled.

Father David stalled a moment before answering. "We have a Christian singles dance next Friday, for 18 through 30. I thought you two could come, to break the ice. I'm sure it'll be like last year, and only have the 25 and under crowd." Father took a long breath. "Oh, and come separately, and walk out together," he added.

"Really?" Quinn asked.

"Yeah, really. I want my chapel booked with weddings this time next year."

Quinn and Ajax laughed.

"Whatever you need, Father," Quinn shimmed, still laughing.

When they got back to Ajax's house, he followed her into the guest room.

"So, what'd you actually say to her?"

Quinn kicked off her shoes by her bag.

"Come on, Ajax, I just said I liked her shoes, and to enjoy her visit."

Ajax squinted his eyes at her.

"Can you leave, so I can change?"

Ajax stood up, but didn't leave. Instead, he walked slowly toward Quinn, backing her into the corner. He put his nose in her hair and growled under his breath.

"You smell ... so ... so ... good."

Quinn didn't quite know what he was up to. So who was she to complain?

Ajax placed his arms around her waist, and bowed a bit. He softly put his lips on hers, but remained stationary. He slowly ran his right hand up her back, and brought the zipper down. He rubbed his hands over her bare skin, and kissed her closed mouth.

"Ajax," Quinn said, a little worried, as Ajax moved his lips to her ear.

"Huh?"

"Ajax?"

Ajax stood up, and took a step back.

"Just wanted to help out with your zipper," he said, smiling.

Quinn didn't return the smile.

"Come on. I was joking. Something about the state you left Katie did something to me," he teased, winking at her, and crossing both hands over his chest.

Quinn shook her head, trying not to laugh.

"Get outta here."

Chapter 36

Quinn didn't return to work, fearful she'd become too tired to keep Dantanian out of her head. Monday, she lounged around her own backyard, trying to keep it up for her mom. Ajax left that morning, to help Father David out with some repairs in the community center hall before the dance. Ajax said there was much to be done before they could have the dance this year. Quinn didn't mind having some time to herself; it hardly happened anymore.

At noon, Quinn wandered in for lunch, and some ice water. It was really warm, when she was out there, working in the sun. She took a pre-made meal from the freezer, removed the lid, and popped it in the microwave. While waiting, she ran to her bathroom to wash up. She decided to rinse off in the shower, and replace her clothes. The ones she had one were drenched in sweat, and covered in soil. When she finished washing up, she changed into a pair of old-school gym shorts, and an active-wear, high=coverage sports bra.

She always wore this in gym, when she attended high school. She hated wearing the normal sports bra in front of all her classmates.

After scarfing down her lunch, she pulled her hair through one of her hats by the door, and headed back to the garden. Last time she texted her mom, she said she wanted to extend the garden another six feet: something to do with wanting to do more canning and freezing, to help with the soup kitchen in the colder months.

Quinn made a beeline for the shed, and started taking out everything she needed to extend the garden. She needed her spade shovel, to remove the grass above the soil, and her rotary cultivator, to break up the soil, when she was finished. Before closing the shed, she grabbed a few wooden stakes, to mark where she was adding on to the garden. After she placed the stakes, she broke ground, and started removing the grass with her shovel, as evenly as she possibly could, and then used the hose to wet down the soil, since it was so dry. By the time she finished, she was drenched and dirty again. She took a quick break, to refill her water glass from the hose, and then resumed her work.

Ajax returned about half past two, dropped his tool bag by Quinn's front door, and took off his heavy work boots and socks.

"Quinn, I'm back. Man, that place was a mess! Still is, but not as bad," he joked.

The house was silent. Ajax made his way to the kitchen, and washed his hands in the sink.

When he was drying his hands, he looked through the window, to find Quinn ripping up the yard near the garden. She was using this thing with teeth on it to tear up the ground. The skin that was uncovered was gleaming with moisture. She was wearing something he might see at a running track, or at the gym. Even though she wasn't thin, to say the least, she was curvy and well-defined from doing factory work for as long as she had. Ajax whistled loudly, and mumbled, "Dang," to himself. Smiling widely, he poured two very large Mason jars of sweetened iced tea, and made his way to the back yard.

"Oh, man, hot, hot, hot!" Ajax said, setting his iced tea down on the patio table.

Quinn stopped spraying water on the ground, turned around, and looked up at the sun.

"Tell me about it. I'm burning up. It's hot out here."

Ajax laughed, and handed her a glass of iced tea.

Quinn quickly drank over half of the tea.

"Yeah, about that: I wasn't talking about the weather, babe."

Quinn smiled at the compliment. "What'll it take to cool you off?" she replied, with a wink.

Ajax was surprised she didn't fall quiet on his cocky compliment. He cleared his throat, and raised his brow. "I can think of a couple things."

Quinn flirtatiously giggled, and downed the rest of the iced tea, handing the glass back to Ajax. "I can, too," she said, as she raised the hose, and pulling the trigger.

Ajax, surprised by Quinn's unpredictable action, lost his footing, and fell back, landing in the mud, with the Mason jar rolling out of his hand, unharmed. Quinn continued spraying him, until he swiped her legs from under her, making her fall. She landed in the soft, muddy, over-watered garden, next to him. They lay there a while, after they finished laughing, to catch their breath. Ajax looked at Quinn; she had lines and spots of mud on her face, and her clothing was about as muddy as his. He smiled at her.

"How do you do it?"

"Do what," she asked.

Ajax smiled, and she returned the smile.

"No matter what you're wearing, or even now, covered in mud, I'm still very attracted to you."

Quinn smiled, even though she felt a little uncomfortable. This would be so much easier, if she knew she wouldn't lose him later.

Quinn sat up, slung the mud off her hands, and turned her gaze to the ground.

"Maybe, for once, you're attracted to someone for more than the physical beauty? 'Cause, Lord knows, I don't compare, nor do I wish to compare, to what sashayed herself though the door of the coffee shop last night."

Ajax fell silent for a moment. He sat up, like he was annoyed. "I won't be making that mistake again."

His hands grabbed each side of her face, and he kissed her, multiple times, softly, on the lips, and then, pushing his body onto hers, making her splat back in the mud. Quinn laughed, grabbed two handfuls of mud, and shoved her arms up his shirt, rubbing the cold mud on his hot skin. His expression made her laugh even harder.

After spraying each other off with the extremely cold hose water, they went inside, and took turns showering. While Ajax was showering, Quinn cooked up some fried chicken and collard green for supper. When Ajax returned to the kitchen, he noticed Quinn was already in her night clothes.

"Yum.   Something smells good," he announced, as he sat down at the table.

Quinn filled the clean Mason jars with ice water, and took them to the table.

"After we eat, I'll clean up, and we can head next door."

Ajax took a drink of the cold, and surprisingly refreshing, water.

"You're the boss," he replied, running his hand through his thick, dark hair.

Quinn dropped the tongs, trying to glance at him.

"I'll get it," he said, picking it up, and washing it off in the sink. "You alright?" he added."

Quinn chuckled uncomfortably. "Uh huh."

Ajax smiled at her cute awkwardness, and grabbed plates from the cupboard, and utensils from the drawer, to set the table.

"Thanks," Quinn mumbled.

After dinner, Quinn cleaned up the kitchen, while Ajax rinsed off the gardening tools from the back yard, and placed them in the shed. When he came back in, Quinn was finished with the dishes. She packed up the leftovers for Ajax's nightly snack. Quinn also took a banana cream pie from the freezer, for something sweet later.

Later that evening, after watching a really bad movie drama Ajax found in a stash of movies in the basement, they went upstairs for snacks. Ajax warmed up the leftovers, and finished them off. Quinn unwrapped the pie, and jumped up to sit on the counter. She didn't even bother slicing it; she dug her fork in, and took a bite.

"Mmm, that's good," She moaned, shoving a forkful of banana cream pie in his mouth.

"Mmm, that is good," he said, coming in closer.

Quinn gave him another bite, and leaned in as if she was going to kiss him, but closed his lower lip between hers.

"Would hate to waste," she smiled sheepishly.

"That was mean," Ajax groaned.

Quinn giggled.

After eating more than half the pie by themselves, then started another movie, but barely made it past opening credit before falling into a food coma, curled close together, his arm around her shoulders.

Chapter 37

The sun sparkled high in the sky, and the weather warm. Quinn sat on her front porch, but she realized she wasn't really at home. She heard the birds chirping, and a light breeze blowing through the trees. She smiled too widely. This was the only place her worries simply faded away.

Quinn looked down the empty street. In the distance, she saw a figure walking toward her. She stood up, walked into the middle of the road, and raised her hand to her forehead to block the sun. In the distance, she could tell the figure was a man. When he walked under the trees that shaded the road, she could see him a lot better. He stood about six feet tall, and had a solid build, with short, dark, curly hair. He had the chin and structure of a superhero. The man stopped about four feet away, and just looked at her, with longing in his eyes. Quinn's breath caught in her chest, when she realized who he was. Quinn stood there, speechless, for a long moment.

"Daddy," she whispered.

He smiled at her, closed the distance, and wrapped her up in his fatherly arms.

"Yes, Sweetheart, it's me. You've turned out to be a strong, confident, young lady, you know that?" he replied.

Quinn hugged him back, as tightly as posable. "How do I miss you this much, even though we've never met?" Quinn asked, muffled in his chest. "I've missed you so," she added.

"We've met, Baby. I watched over you from the day you were born. When you were little, you always seemed to sense me," he said, kissing her on the top of her head.

After an extremely long hug, Quinn reluctantly took a step back, to look at her dad.

"You look so much like me, Quinn. Your pretty face you must get from your mother."

Quinn smiled, more from her excitement to have him close, than his fatherly compliment. Her dad was so handsome. He looked the same as he did in the pictures that hung in her home. He hadn't aged since the day he died.

"Dad, how did you die?" Quinn asked, her smile fading.

Her dad looked at her with a soft smile, and moved a hair from her face.

"I gave my life to save a mother and her unborn child."

Quinn gasped in shock, but before she could say anything, he added, "Not you and your mom, Honey. I was coming back from transferring an inmate to another jail. We stopped at a gas station. I walked into a robbery, and the guy who was holding up the store, he became startled, and pointed his gun at a very young woman, who was standing near the door. I didn't have time to think; I just jumped in front of her, and he pulled the trigger."

Quinn stood quietly, and a single tear escaped her eye. "Why did you do it, Daddy?"

"'Cause I would've wanted someone to do the same for your mom, if she was in the same situation. Truthfully, I didn't even think; I just did it."

Quinn looked at him. He looked so proud and confident.

"As much as I wish I could say you shouldn't have, I can't. Daddy, you saved two lives, knowing you would lose your family."

Her dad smiled. "I never lost my family; I'm always there with you and your mom."

After a moment, they sat on the porch together. Her dad sat hunched, with his elbows on his knees, and his hands twined together under his chin. It looked like he was doing some serious thinking.

"Have you decided what you're gonna do about Ajax's situation?"

Quinn turned her body to face her dad's. "Yeah, surprisingly, I think I have."

Her dad gave a soft smile. "Well, what's your plan?" he asked.

"It wouldn't be a surprise, if I told you, now would it? Anywho, it's not like you all up here don't know. Most likely, you know everything I do, before I do it."

Quinn's dad looked puzzled. "Sweet girl, this is all on you. The thing with free will, and all. Even the Big Guy doesn't dig through your head. Although, at this moment, and as a worried dad, I wish I did. I wish I could just keep you here with me till it's all over."

Quinn frowned at him. "Daddy, I dreamed of Ajax dying. I'm not sure if I can help him; all I we seem to be doing is prolonging. My plans aren't shocking or heroic." Quinn paused for a moment. "I don't know how I'll recover, when I do lose him, Daddy," She added.

"It won't be easy, Baby," he said, looking down at his feet. "There's always a loophole," he whispered. "Just keep running, if you need to," he added.

It pained Quinn to see the hurt on his face, knowing the end result would be painful for his daughter.

Quinn and her dad talked for hours. She didn't need to catch him up on her life, because he knew everything, from every scrap from her childhood, her hormonal teen years and her first love, Ajax. He told her stories from when he and her mom dated, and how he felt on his wedding day. Quinn's favorite was how excited he was that they were having a baby. He knew it was a girl the day her mom told him. He named her Quinn that day. When he told the story, his eyes were so bright, and his smile could easily split his cheeks. Quinn just listened, and took in his presence, scared she wouldn't feel this way again.

Quinn blew out a breath of air, and shrugged her shoulders. "There'res a lot of things on my mind, Daddy."

Quinn's father tilted his head, and blew out a breath of his own. "Everything'll be as it should. Sometimes, all we can do is sit back, and enjoy what we have, while we have it."

Quinn yawned lightly. "I know."

Quinn's dad wrapped his arm around her shoulder, and pulled her in. She laid her head on his chest. She felt awfully tired. The comfort of her father's touch, and the sense of safety she received from him, had her so relaxed; she fell into a peaceful sleep.

When she woke up, she was alone in the room she fell asleep in. The room was still dark, but she could see the sun shining through the window, from outside Ajax's bedroom door. She knew it was still early. She heard water running in the pipes, meaning Ajax must be in the shower. She lay back down, closed her eyes, and thought about the encounter she had just had with her dad, and all the stuff they talked about.

She must have fallen back to sleep, because when she woke up, she was sitting in a familiar field, beside the beautiful angel.

"How was it to meet your father?"

Quinn smiled sweetly at Michael. "Unexpected, and I enjoyed every minute I had with him."

The angel smiled, and nodded with understanding.

"It's so lovely here," Quinn whispered, more to herself.

"Quinn," Michael said her name with purpose, but paused. "On this side, we can feel that darkness closing in, and our time is running out. The future I see still remains the same."

The angel raised his arm, and swiped it at the earth in front of them. Quinn no longer looked at the heavenly landscape she'd just admired; now, she looked at the same wooded area where she'd watched Ajax die twice before. Quinn's breath hitched, as she saw Ajax running toward them.

"Calm, child, this is not real at the moment," Michael said, patting her shoulders.

Quinn watched intently. From one side she saw herself, farther away. When Ajax stopped running, it wasn't long before a dagger was shoved in his back. This time, she didn't make it to him, so he could die in her arms. Instead, she watched as Dantanian closed in on Quinn. The seen ended there.

"How do we have the same outcome, but worse?" Quinn asked, breathing heavy. "I realize what I need to do. I figured you knew. Dad told me God doesn't take information, because of free will and all," she added.

The angel cleared his throat. "I understand you have a plan, and I pray that, when the time comes, I can give you strength to help in any way

I can. At the moment, our outcome doesn't look promising."

After a very long, tiring pause, he added, "I'm only ordered to protect you from Dantanian, or any evil that comes from hell. I can't protect you from the evil that humans are capable of."

Quinn didn't respond, but her head was spinning with all the information he had just given her. Quinn's eyes became large, as if coming across a new discovery.

"Oh," was all she said.

Chapter 38

Quinn woke later in the morning, long after Ajax left to help Father David with the on-going repairs they were doing, before the singles' dance next Friday. Before Quinn headed to her back yard, she called and ordered some Tuscany tumbled pavers, for the walkway through the garden, and some eight-by-eight red bricks, to put around the garden. The delivery guy said he'd have it out to the house before noon.

Before the bricks could be set, she had to dig a trench around the garden, in which to put the red bricks, and smooth out and flatten the dirt, to put down the walking path of Tuscany tumbled pavers. By the time the bricks were delivered, Quinn had the garden prepped. She set the bricks and pavers,, and she was finished with the garden by one-thirty in the afternoon.

Quinn went inside, and washed her hands and face, which were caked with dirt and mud. She looked at herself in the mirror; her tank top and short overalls were a mess, too.

"Well, since I'm already dirty, maybe I'll pick up some cleaning supplies, and help the guys with the cleanup," she thought.

After grabbing some cleaning items, she picked up a couple of pizzas and pop for a late lunch. When she arrived at the hall, her arms were full, and she kicked the door, hoping someone would come and open it. After a few harsh kicks to the door, Father David opened it, smiled, looked over his shoulder, and called out, "Food!" Father David grabbed the food and drink, and moved out of the way, so Quinn could enter.

"I thought I'd feed y'all, and help ya clean up some, since I finished Mom's garden project," Quinn said, setting the cleaning stuff in the corner of the pretty large hall.

"Thanks, we can use the extra help," Father David said, setting the food down on the only table in the room.

Ajax came trotting out backwards, removing a shirt that was drenched in dirt and sweat, and tossing it by his overflowing toolbox.

"Ajax, if you want, you can use the hose to clean up in the back. The hose is in the alley, where we parked," Father David said, not looking up from setting the table. Quinn stood there, trying her hardest not to stare at him.

"Hey, Quinn, while I clean up, would you grab me a clean shirt out of the car?" Ajax asked, making his way to the exit in the back.

All Quinn did was nod.

Quinn opened the back door to Father David's SUV, and grabbed a sleeveless, black tee, and a hand towel, which was on top of the bag; she tossed the towel over her shoulder. When she turned around to shut the door, Ajax was right there; Quinn jumped. Ajax smiled, and took the towel from her shoulder.

"Sorry," he said, smiling.

"No, you're not," Quinn responded.

Quinn watched Ajax dry off, and put the shirt on. It wasn't like she could go anywhere, if she wanted to; he was still standing right there, blocking her.

"Did you walk here with all that stuff?" he asked.

Quinn nodded.

"I left my keys right by the door; take 'em next time, okay?"

Again, Quinn nodded.

Ajax smiled. "You alright?"

Quinn really didn't know what to say; nothing seemed worth saying. So, she gave up, gave him a kiss, and hugged him.

"What's that for?"

Quinn really wanted to tell him about her dreams: about her dad, and what Archangel Michael had to say, but she knew she shouldn't right now.

"Just 'cause," she replied.

Ajax smiled and returned her kiss, with a few pecks of his own.

"Just 'cause works for me, Baby," he said, winking.

Ajax wrapped the damp towel around her neck, and pulled her in for another small, but sweet, kiss. "Now, let's go chow down," he added.

Quinn smiled and snapped the towel on his rear, when he turned to walk away.

"Ouch," he said, not even turning around.

After everyone ate, the guys got back to whatever they'd been doing before she got there, and Quinn did some major dusting. She cleaned all the windows, and cleaned both of the bathrooms, before taking a break. Sweating as badly as she was, she had to look like a drowned rat. She walked through the exit, to get to the hose. After she let the water run for a minute, she drank fast, until she was panting. She calmed her breathing, and then rinsed her hair, which was a knotted mess, and wrung it out, and then put it back up. When she turned around, there was a guy leaning against the fence. He was a clean kind of handsome. He had short hair and a close shave. He wore black dress slacks, a lime-green button-down dress shirt, with a dark green tie, and he had a suit jacket hanging over his left arm. Quinn stood there for a moment.

"You waiting for someone?" she asked, a little uneasy, and keeping her distance.

"Nah, not really. Although I wouldn't mind waiting for you," he said, smiling.

Quinn shook her head, quite uncomfortable, and backed herself to the door.

"Aw, was it something I said," the guy teased. "Here, give this to Ajax, when you see him," he said, handing her a folded letter. "He never seems too far away from you," he added, chuckling.

Before Quinn could respond, the back door opened with a screech, making her jump.

"Everything alright," Father David asked Quinn, his eyes darting from the man and back to her.

Quinn nodded.

"Yes, Padre, I was just leaving," the guy said, looking at Quinn. "I'll see ya around, Quinn," he added, as he walked away.

After the guy was out of sight, Quinn followed Father David inside.

"Who was that," he asked.

Quinn shrugged her shoulders. "I dunno, but he left something for Ajax."

Father David pointed to the right hand side of the building, toward a long hall. "He's down there, if you want to take it to him."

Quinn slowly walked across the large room, and made her way down the hall. She didn't pay any mind to her surrounding, until a hand grabbed her around the waist from behind, covered her mouth, and lifted her right off the ground, into a room off to the side. In panic, Quinn kicked and jerked around. After only a second, the hands let go of her.

"Quinn, chill, it's me," Ajax said, smirking.

Quinn pushed him hard. She was shaken up; her hands were so shaky, she lost feeling in them.

"It's not funny," she said in a quivering voice.

Ajax's smile dropped from his face, when he realized how frightened she was.   He lifted his palms in front of him.

"I'm sorry, Babe; I didn't mean to scare you. I saw you coming, and I could've sworn you saw me."

Ajax closed the gap between them, and hugged her.

"Someone came to visit you," Quinn said, stepping back, and handing him the note.

Ajax took it, opened it, and read it out loud.

> *Ajax*
>
> *Hey, Bud. I'm in town. Kate dragged me with her. I'd like to get together before I leave her ass here. Not sure why she had me come. She knows I got an education, so I wouldn't have to deal with crap like this. Well, my number's down below. I have some interesting information you may want.*
>
> *Later.*

"You know him?" Quinn asked.

Ajax folded the paper, and shoved it into his pocket. "Yeah, Max. He helped keep me on the clean part of my dad's jobs. He isn't a part of the family biz. He's actually an owner of multiple five-star hotels.   For the last year, he's been traveling, and hasn't been anywhere near his family, except his sister, Kate," he said, making eye contact with Quinn.

"Is he the one who has you all in a muck?"

Quinn didn't respond, but she was a lot calmer.

"He wouldn't have acted like that, if he knew what my father and his men had done. He's cocky, and too confident, but harmless," he said.

Quinn smiled and nodded.

"Now can I do what I had in mind?"

Quinn smiled again, as he backed her up against the door, which he'd shut after grabbing her from the hall. Ajax bent down, and kissed her, sweetly, on the lips, keeping his hands on the door.

"Couldn't just do that with the father lurking."

Quinn giggled, and pulled his face in for another kiss.

"Yum," Ajax said, raising his brows.

"What do you say we call it a day, and go home and shower. I'll order some food, and give Max a call, and see what info he has for us.

Chapter 39

Ajax waited on the food while Quinn was in the shower, and when it arrived, Max walked up with the delivery boy. Ajax paid the kid, and shut the door after Max came in.

"Dude, that wasn't cool, startling Quinn like that. When unknown people show up, unannounced, around here, she ends up getting hurt."

Max raised his arms in a defensive gesture. "Dude, I was trying to flirt, not scare."

"Don't do that, either, Man," Ajax said, less seriously this time.

Ajax and Max carried plates and silverware to the living room, where they sat and talked over a couple of beers before eating.

When Quinn left the bathroom, she overheard Ajax and Max talking. Max told Ajax something about how whatever Kate says wasn't information he wants to go by.

"Your dad doesn't want you home, unless it's in a body bag," Max said in a hushed tone.

Quinn made it known that she was in earshot, when she shut the guest bedroom door. She walked into the kitchen from the other side, grabbed herself a glass of iced tea, and the rest of the package of beer, which was on the counter, and took them into the living room.

"How was the shower?" Ajax asked, when she walked in.

"Wet," she said with a smile.

Max stood up, and reached out his hand. "I'm Max. Sorry I startled you earlier."

"Forgiven," she said, shaking his hand, after putting down the drinks.

Quinn sat on the floor, in front of the coffee table, and started opening the boxes of food. Ajax had ordered BBQ and the fixings. After everyone made a plate, Max took a beer, handed one to Ajax, and then shoved one toward Quinn. Quinn shook her head. Ajax leaned over, and pulled the beer over to himself.

Dinner continued smoothly; the guys seemed to enjoy themselves. Quinn realized Ajax was right: the guy was cocky, but not a jerk. She listened to them take a trip down memory lane. Quinn couldn't believe the life Ajax had lived before she got to know him. They talked about their not-so-normal teen years, Even though it seemed out of the normal, they made the best of it, maybe more than they should have, at some points in their stories. She sat back, and listened for a couple of hours, before Max announced that he had to head out-of-town tonight, to make it to a scheduled meeting on the other side of the country. Max said his farewell to Ajax, with a hug and a knuckle bump.

"It was such a pleasure meeting you, Quinn," Max said, giving her a quick side hug. "You've gotta be the first person to take a low blow at my sister," he said, laughing. "The first temper tantrum I actually enjoyed," he added, walking out the door.

"What low blow?" Ajax asked, looking at her as he closed the door.

"I'm not sure what he was talking about," Quinn said, smiling, as she walked back into the living room.

After Quinn finished up the dishes, she plopped on the couch with Ajax.

"Hey," he said, twining his fingers with hers.

"Hey," Quinn responded, followed by a yawn.

"Wanna go to bed?"

"Whenever you're ready," Quinn said, yawning.

"Come on," Ajax said. He pulled her to her feet.

He led her around the house, shutting down and locking up, before they headed down the stars. Quinn didn't even bother turning on the lights; she just fell on Ajax's side of the bed, and scooted over to the side she'd claimed.

"Why don't you just bring your bag down here? You haven't even slept in the guest room," Ajax whispered against the back of her head. Ajax almost thought she'd fallen asleep already.

"I dunno," she said softly. "It's personal, like leaving a toothbrush at someone's place," she added.

"What would be wrong about you leaving it at my place?" Ajax asked, seriously.

Quinn was silent for a moment, before she turned around to face him. His face was serious.

"Can I ask you something?,"

Ajax nodded

"What would you call what we have,?

Ajax didn't hesitate. "A relationship."

Quinn held back her surprise.

"Do you think this is anything less than a relationship?" Ajax asked, a little hurt. "What relationships have you been in?" he asked.

"A couple short ones, but they all end the same," Quinn said.

"Why did they end?"

Quinn felt a little irritated at the moment, but mostly at herself. "What do you think would ruin teen relationship?" Quinn asked, trying not to roll her eyes.

When Ajax didn't answer, Quinn sat up, and faced him. She really wanted this to be over quickly. "Listen, Ajax, when a relationship gets so far, then the other person notices it's been derailed for any further physical advancements, and it's a huge killer of relationships."

Ajax hung his head, and ran his hand through his hair, before making eye contact. "Last I checked, I'm not a teenager, and I'm not looking for advancement. I... I'm... I want something real. Besides, being in your presence, and the way you look at me the way you do, everything else is just perks."

Quinn couldn't help but blush. Then, she thought of her dreams of losing him, and the sadness was painful. She ran everything through her head at high speed. What if she lost him before ever really knowing, loving, or accepting him? Wouldn't that be harder? Would she regret it?

"Hey, come on, don't leave me hanging on my own words. I'm starting to feel like a fool here," Ajax said, with a tilt of his head.

Quinn stood up, and left the room. Ajax stumbled, trying to catch up, but by the time he got to the landing of the staircase, she was at the top, with her bag in hand. A look of relief crossed his face.

Quinn slowly walked down the stars. When she was at just below eye level, she asked, "Are you sure? I'm all in, as long as you know my heart is on the line."

Ajax took her bag, and dropped it at his feet. "All in," he said, his breath a little loud. "My heart has been on the line since the day we picked up broken glass together."

Ajax put his arms around her waist, and gave her a kiss on the lips. Then he walked away with her bag. Quinn walked into the bedroom, and sat on the loveseat at the foot of the bed. After Ajax put her bag down, he joined her.

"Wanna go back to bed?" he asked.

Quinn shook her head. Ajax sat by her, and blew out a burst of air he'd been holding. Quinn turned toward him, a little nervously, and kissed him sweetly. She noticed that, whenever they kissed each other, his eyes never closed.

"Why do you keep your eyes open?" she asked.

Ajax grunted a very irresistible laugh. "Hard to see the beauty in front of me, if my eyes are closed."

Quinn blushed again, but didn't hide it. She leaned in to his mouth, and kissed him again. Ajax returned the kiss on her lips, cheeks, and chin. When he returned to her mouth, she opened her mouth slightly, and caught his lower lip softly. If Ajax was surprised, he didn't let on. He let her make the first attempt, just in case that wasn't meant to happen. Again, Quinn's mouth opened slightly, kissed him again, and, this time, they entered a full-on kiss, but still no tongue. Ajax pulled Quinn onto his lap; he noticed she was a little shaky. He reached back, and pulled the hair tie from her hair. Quinn kissed him again; this time she ran the tip of her tongue along his lower lip, making him pull her in for a closer kiss. When he had his mouth on hers, he pulled his head back about an inch.

"You're shaking. Why?"

Quinn didn't realize she was, until just then, and that just made it worse. "Nervous and excited," she said, with a light giggle.

"Wanna get under the covers?" Ajax asked.

Quinn wasn't sure what he was asking.

"First base, only," he assured her, smiling smugly.

Ajax stood up, and let Quinn slide down. They made their way to the bed, lay on their sides, face-to-face, and covered up. Ajax scooted as close to her as he could get, and ran his hand up and down her clothed back. This time, Ajax leaned in, and grabbed her mouth with his. This sent a tingling shock through Quinn. The nervousness turned to crazed butterflies. Quinn's body let out a soft moan, without notifying her first. This seemed to make the kiss intensify. Quinn found it hard to keep up, and she really tried. Quinn broke the kiss, softly, to catch her breath. Ajax didn't need a breather; he kept his lips on her. He traveled from her cheek to her chin, down her chin to her neck and from her neck to her ear, which caused another moan. Again, the moan set off another signal to Ajax, and he came right back to her mouth. Quinn was in complete bliss. She ran her hands up and down his bare chest and side. His body was warm to the touch. Quinn slid her lips from his mouth to his neck, and to his ear. He let out a growl, which lit a fire in the pit of Quinn's belly. Ajax used his body to push her over to her back, and settled his weight on top of her. His lips didn't leave her mouth, as he maneuvered himself over her, without inflicting any embarrassing pain. Somehow, he landed in the best position ever. Every time he moved his lips, or took a deep breath, every nerve in her body flared.   After a long time, which she couldn't count, she had to speak.

"I really don't wanna say this, but we should chill.   I could really use a really cold shower," Quinn said, out of breath.

Ajax laughed, brushing hair from her face, and kissing her brow.   "You and me both, Babe," he said, still laughing.

"Wow," Quinn breathed.

Ajax smiled at her.

That night they fell asleep in each other's arms.

Chapter 40

The wind coming in through the window sent goosebumps multiplying up and down her arms. Quinn hit the button, and the windows rolled up. She was on her way home from work, after working a long, dreadful, double shift. She couldn't wait to get home, to shower and get some well-deserved sleep. Quinn had to take the long route home, because of all the construction happening downtown. She kept herself alert and awake by listening to some loud classic rock, and sipping cold pop through a straw.

After a few minutes, Quinn saw the bridge ahead, and felt relieved, because, after she crosses the bridge, she was only a few blocks from home. She stepped on the brake, to slow down, as the sign read, but her brakes weren't working. She pressed them to the floor, and still nothing. Not a big deal: the roads were empty this time of night, and she'd had this issue a couple times before. She'd learned how to slow down enough to control the car. The center of the bridge was up-hill.

"That'll help," she thought.

Just as she entered the bridge, a man came out of nowhere, and Quinn swerved to miss him. Going 55 miles per hour, she broke through the thin, wooden rails, and went nose-first into the wintery, ice-cold water below. Once the car hit, it didn't take long for the water to start seeping through the vents and cracks of the car. Quinn tried rolling down her window as soon as the car landed, but the windows wouldn't budge — not one of them. She struggled against the seatbelt, but it was stuck, too. It was like something was blocking her attempt. Just before the water filled her lungs, she saw a dark, menacing figure in her backseat. When the light came to her, the darkness vanished.

Quinn woke up coughing, her eyes flew open, and she saw the dark figure from her dream. Dantanian lay over her, with a grin that oozed with darkness. Quinn turned her head, to find she was on her own with him. She opened her mouth to scream, but he laid his palm on her chest, and her voice muted.

"Quinn, my darling angel," he chuckled. "I can be who you really want; why would you chose someone you can't keep?" he asked, with mock sadness.

Dantanian nodded his head, and the world around them blurred. When her vision corrected, he wasn't Dantanian anymore; he was, but he looked just like Ajax.

"See, I can be him. Hell, I can be anyone I want, or anyone you want me to be," he said, winking in Ajax's skin.

Dantanian moved his hand from her chest slightly.

"You're disgusting," she spat, in a horrified whispered.

Dantanian blurred again, and now he looked like an actual demon from nightmares. His face dripped with black acid-like goop. His eyes were red and black, and he had a snake-like tongue. Quinn closed her eyes, and gained strength from a powerful force; somehow, she freed herself from beneath him. She didn't bother looking back; she ran out of the bedroom, up the stars, into the kitchen, and right into Ajax's arms, knocking him against the counter.

"He's here! Dantanian's here!" Quinn said, pointing.

She paused, turned toward Ajax again, and stepped back. Dantanian, in Ajax's body, took a step toward her, and grinned; his face was rested and scary, even though he looked like Ajax.

"Dantanian," she whispered.

When he reached to grab her, she screamed, and almost fell to the floor in fear. Quinn turned, and high-tailed it out of the kitchen. She ran down the hall, to the front door. Right before she got to the door, it swung open, and there Ajax stood, smiling.

"Hey, Babe," he said, putting his keys down.

"Get away from me!" she screamed at him this time. She had no intention of being fooled again.

"Hey, what did I do?" he asked, looking genuinely concerned.

Quinn trembled with fear. She shook her head back and forth. She reached her hand to her chest, but the cross was gone. Tears started trickling down her face. Ajax took a step closer, out of concern.

"Don't touch me, Dantanian!" she yelled, her voice cracking.

Ajax looked at her, confused, and then he looked past her, but didn't see anything.

"Quinn. Baby, if you believe I'm not me, or believe I'm Dantanian, please walk past me, and out the front door."

Quinn, with silent tears running down her face, moved slowly around Ajax, scared he would grab her, but he didn't, and she walked out the front door. Once outside, she turned around, to see Ajax standing where she'd left him, but now he was turned in her direction. He looked very worried. Quinn wasn't sure what she should do. He could be anyone right now. Where would she be safe?

"Quinn, it's really me."

Quinn, still shaking, wanted to believe him. "Then go downstairs, get my cross, and come back to the door."

Ajax didn't hesitate, and he was back in less than a minute.

"Slide the front up and touch it."

Ajax did as she said, and nothing happened. Then she watched him close it, walk outside, and placed it around her neck.

Quinn wrapped her arms around him, and all she felt was relief.

"Are you alright? Did he hurt you?" Ajax asked in an angry voice.

"No. He just scared me. I ran from him, and saw you in the kitchen. It wasn't you, it was him.... he...." She lost her words, as she started getting frantic again. "He's the one that ran me off the bridge last year," she added.

Ajax eased her back a little. "That was before I came back to town, Quinn."

Quinn nodded, and shrugged her shoulders.

Ajax's mouth was agape; he shook his head. "Wanna back out of helping Father David today?"

Quinn shook her head, and mumbled, "No, let's get dressed and go help."

Ajax kissed the top of her head. "Come on, let's grab coffee on the way?"

While Ajax and Father David worked on the hall, Quinn spent the day in the church. Church was where she felt the safest. She prayed most of the morning and afternoon. After all the praying, she felt a lot better, and knew she was stronger in every way. With strength on her side, she left the safety of the church, and went to pick up lunch for herself and the guys.

Across the street, at the coffee shop, while she was waiting on her order, Katie swayed herself through the door. Quinn ignored her entrance, and sipped the coffee she'd been given.

"So, I hear there's a singles' dance next Friday," Katie said, from beside Quinn.

"Yep," Quinn responded.

"I think that'd be totally fun to attend."

Quinn turned around, and smiled a sweet smile. "You're more than welcome to come. You'd learn so much at a Christian singles' dance."

Katie turned on her overly pointed heels, and clucked her tongue. "I may learn how to get my boyfriend back."

Quinn didn't flinch at her remark. "Or, you'll meet a nice, God-fearing man, who'll teach you manners, respect, and a little self-control and self-confidence," Quinn said, without any sarcasm. "I really hope this happens for you one day. You're so much more than you show people," Quinn added.

Katie didn't say anything more. She retrieved her order, and left the coffee shop. Quinn was pleased with herself for being decent, even though it took everything in her to do so.

After the food was boxed and bagged up, she took everything to the hall, where she was greeted by two hungry men; one of them showed appreciation by a quick kiss on the lips. They both looked a sweaty mess, but the place looked so much better. After lunch was finished, Quinn cleaned up the floors, and then sat and waited. She couldn't believe, after what happened this morning, she felt so calm. She wasn't scared of not knowing whether anyone was who they said they were. Deep down, she could sense whether the demon was around. Her prayers must have been heard, loud and clear. Everything felt different to her. Her senses were more alive and accountable. It seemed almost like her eyes had always been closed, and now were opened.

The rest of the week flew by without incident.

On Wednesday, Quinn got an email from her mom, informing her that she'd be home Friday night.

After Ajax and Quinn finished up at the hall with Father David on Friday, they ate an early dinner out. Later, they both did some grocery shopping, before their moms returned. After they helped each other put away the food they'd bought, they sat on Quinn's front porch. Ajax sat on the lower step, in front of Quinn, who was rubbing her hand playfully on the stubble on the sides of his cheeks.

"Can you fathom that, in a couple more days, the hall will be finished?"

Quinn stopped messing with his cheeks, and wrapped her arms around his neck; she set her chin on his shoulder.

"I'm extremely happy it's almost done. It's been a lot of work. Speaking of work, I have to go back to work on Monday."

Ajax stroked his hands over hers. "Save a dance for me on Friday?"

Quinn giggled, and kissed his cheek. "Only if you like being stepped on."

Ajax turned around, and kissed her lips softly. "Only if you're the one stepping on me." Ajax kissed her again wrapping his arms loosely around her waist.

"You gonna be okay without me here?" he asked, between kisses.

"No, but I'll pretend," she replied with a fake pout. "Hey, look, we still have an hour before they get here. I'm thirsty for some iced tea. Want some tea or a beer?"

Ajax agreed, and followed her in.

Quinn opened a beer for Ajax, and handed it to him; she poured herself a glass of tea. She leaned against the counter, and enjoyed the crisp iced tea she was drinking. Ajax finished his beer as he rested, his back to the wall. They looked at each other for the longest time, without saying anything. Ajax pushed himself off the wall, set his bottle on the counter near Quinn, and sidestepped in front of her. He took the glass from her hand, and set in next to the bottle. He put his hands on the counter behind her, leaned in, and gave her a kiss, as he lifted her onto the counter.

"What're your plans for tomorrow?" he asked.

Quinn could smell the sweetness from his beer, as he spoke.

"I was hoping that, while you're working with Father David, with the decorations, I'd go shopping for a dress, with Mom, and maybe bring y'all some lunch, or something."

Ajax straightened up, and moved in, between her knees. "Good. I already miss ya." Ajax paused for a moment. "These cell phone things that we never seem to use … if you need me, just text or call. I'm a click away."

Quinn nodded her head. "Can I text or call, 'cause I wanna?"

Ajax kissed her forehead. "Even better, Babe."

For the next 30 minutes, they chatted, but mostly, blissfully, made out, until they heard the sound of jangling keys outside the door.

"Later, Babe," Ajax said, going out the back door, leaving Quinn smiling on the countertop.

"Guess he missed his mom, too," she whispered to herself.

When the door swung open, Quinn jumped off the counter, ran to her mom, and hugged her tightly for several seconds.

"Mom, I missed you so much!"

Quinn's mom held her at arm's reach, and looked her over.

"I missed my pretty girl, too. Lemme get this stuff to my room, and we need to catch up."

Quinn and her mom took her stuff to her room, and then went to the kitchen, where Quinn poured another cup of tea, for her mom, and handed it to her.

"So, you did some work in the garden?" her mom asked.

"Sure did! Wanna see?" Quinn asked.

Quinn turned on all the back door lights. Because they spent so much time in the garden, they had enough light in the back yard to be out in their backyard at all hours.   Quinn's mom followed her out the back door, and past the patio.

"Wow, you really extended the garden.   Did you hire someone to do all this work, or have someone help?" her mom asked.

"Nope, did it all by myself.   Although I did have the bricks delivered."

"I love it. Quinn, that's some great work."

Quinn pecked her mom's cheek.

"So what're your plans for the weekend?" her mom asked.

"I thought it'd be fun if we went dress shopping.   Father David begged us to attend the singles' dance."

Quinn's mom smiled to herself.   "Sure, shopping sounds fun. You going with Ajax?"

Quinn nodded, making her mother grin a little more. Quinn understood her mom had questions, but Quinn didn't want to get into it tonight.

"So, how was the singles' cruise, Mom?" she asked, leading her back into the house, turning off the backyard lights, and locking up behind them.

"It was fun. Although, the men were dull."

Quinn laughed at her mom's response. "Since that didn't work out, you're always welcome to join us for the singles' dance," Quinn said laughing.

"Nu-uh, no way.   This lady's done with anything having the word single in it," she chuckled.   "Still, I can't believe Father David talked us into it.   He has some kind of mind power, that man," she added, scrunching her nose.

Quinn laughed at her expression. "Yeah, I'm starting to think so, too."

A couple of hours later after her mom turned in for the night, Quinn lounged in a nice, hot bubble bath.   Ever since she spent time in the chapel, praying, she'd had a clearer mind.   Quinn relaxed, and laid her head back on the cool, porcelain tub.   She cleared her mind, and listened. When her eyes opened again, she knew Michael had been helping her sense what was and wasn't really what or who they seemed.   When the water started to cool off, she stood up, and toweled off. She put on her pajamas, and pulled her hair from the hair tie, laying it on the counter.   Quinn brushed her teeth, and shut off the bathroom light, before climbing into her bed.   After she got nice and comfortable, she plucked her phone from the nightstand, and a text from Ajax awaited her.

> *I miss you already.   I hope you're enjoying some time with your mom.   I understand how much you missed her.   As soon as my mom came in, she had to tell me how crazy the selection was on the singles cruise. She told me all this before even giving me a hug.   I tell you, this woman wasn't happy with the singles that were stocked on the*

> *ship.   She did say the food was worth it,
> though.*

Quinn smiled, and hit reply.

> *I miss you too.*

She hit *send*, and typed again:

> *Mom went to bed not too long ago.   She
> didn't seem too happy with the selection of
> men, either.   I'm starting to think they
> missed their crime shows.   No man can
> come close to the ones on the shows they
> watch.*

Smiling, she typed a third message.

> *Mom loved the extended garden I put in for
> her.   It won't be long before she has the
> whole backyard filled with veggies for the
> fall.   I, myself, look forward to doing that,
> as well.   Ya know, without you here, the
> surrounding space is void.   We have spent
> so much time together, it feels normal.*

Quinn pushed *send*, got up to fill her glass
with water from the bathroom sink, and laid back
down.   After a few minutes, her phone vibrated on
her nightstand.   She opened the message, and it
read:

I know exactly what you mean. Although I'm not sure I could've said it as well as you. Mom made me tell her everything we've been up to. No worries, I did leave out some stuff. Haha. My mom's happy to hear we're "courting." She said your mom predicted it. So, are we "courting," Babe?

Quinn blushed, and replied again.

My mom wished it since the diner we all had together, I think. Truth be told, I wasn't sure how I felt. The feelings were all new. I really didn't know how I felt, till I woke up from that fever. I could hear and sense you the whole time. Enough about that. I know how I feel now. Over text is not a way I want to share my feeling.

I still miss you.

Quinn hit *send*, and waited. It didn't take long before her phone vibrated again. She opened it to a one-liner.

Come to your back door.

Quinn dropped her phone, and jumped out of bed. For some reason, she had the old excitement that Christmas morning brought when she was a child. When she swung open the back door, Ajax was standing about ten feet away.

"Took you long enough," he said, smiling.

Quinn didn't respond; she just ran into his embrace. She didn't realize she missed him this much, after only a few hours. She hadn't spent an evening without him in weeks. Ajax bent, and gave her a long, sweet kiss. The kiss didn't end until they could no longer keep their eyes open, and had to part ways.

Chapter 42

"I absolutely like this one, Mom," Quinn called out, behind the solid cream, black, and silver curtains.

Quinn came out, and looked in the triple mirror the store had set up for full viewing.

"Oh, wow. That looks like something Audrey Hepburn would've worn in the mid-1960s," her mom said, from behind her.

The dress was vintage style, and the color of brushed bronze, with a scooped neckline, which zipped up the back. It was made of lace, with a mildly fluffy skirt, which fell to the knee.

"This is the one," Quinn said, looking at her mom in the mirror.

"Good choice. You have good taste."

"Just luck. I fell in love with the $30 price tag first," Quinn said, walking back into the changing room, laughing. "It's like 70 percent off today," she added.

Before leaving the store, Quinn bought a pair of shoes, with a two-inch heel, which, unbelievably, matched the dress perfectly.

After Quinn purchased her dress, they went out for lunch, and sat and talked until about one in the afternoon. Quinn's mom headed home with the dress, saying she was in desperate need of a late afternoon nap. Quinn stayed in town, and grabbed a box of tacos, and water, and took them to the hall.

At the hall, Father David and Ajax were finishing up the last of the work. They'd thought they needed another day or two, but now would be able to bust it out, quite quickly, today. They should be completely finished by six.

"Where's Quinn," Father David asked.

"She wanted to hang out with her mom, and get a dress for the dance. She might swing by with lunch, if she has time. I hope she brings that dress, so I can see it."

"Ajax, just a little advice: wait until the dance to see it. That's the best part."

"In your line of work, how is it that you're a romantic?" Ajax asked, raising his brows.

"I wasn't always a man of the cloths," Father David said, tilting his head to the side, like he was cool. Then he laughed at himself. "Actually, I do some couples' counseling, and I get to hear both sides," he added.

"Stud," Ajax said, rolling his eyes.

Father David was about to shoulder bump him, but they heard Quinn yell, "Food!"

Father David smiled. "Saved by the girl."

Ajax just laughed and rolled his eyes.

It didn't take long for Father David and Ajax to come barreling in.

"I was almost frightened that you wouldn't come feed us today," Father David said, giving her a quick hug, and taking the food from her.

"I wouldn't dream of letting two of my favorite guys go hungry." Quinn, left standing there with her emptied arms still out, nodding her head.

"I can fill those empty arms," Ajax said, walking into her waiting embrace.

Ajax took a deep breath. She smelled the same as always, but it was much stronger, and the light surrounding her seemed a little brighter than normal.

"May I kiss you?" Ajax whispered.

"I would be upset if you didn't," Quinn responded.

Ajax smiled, and gave her a sweet kiss on the lips. "Wouldn't want you upset not would we?" he said, dragging her to the table.

Quinn sat and watched them eat, laughing at how badly they teased and joked around each other. What caught Quinn's attention was how Ajax's glow was brighter today. She tried not to stare, so when she did look at him, she just smiled. When they told her they'd be done at eight that evening, Quinn was over the moon happy. Maybe they could find something to do around town, sometime after he got off.

After everyone ate, Quinn pulled Ajax aside, close to the doors. "Thanks for dropping by last night. That's exactly what I needed," Quinn said quietly.

Ajax used his finger to move a few curls from her face. "Trust me, it was out of complete selfishness," he admitted, with a wink and a drop-dead, dreamy smile.

Quinn gave him a peck on the mouth. "In that case, be selfish all you want."

Ajax raised his brow, and intensely eyed her. "Oh, really, now?" he asked teasingly.

"Uh huh," Quinn nodded, trying not to giggle at his expression.

"You might regret saying that later," he said slowly, taking her out the front door.

Quinn laughed out loud, and blushed. "I sure hope so."

Once outside, Ajax leaned in for a very long, wet kiss. His hand glided softly over her back, leaving chills and goosebumps in their wake. "Any regrets yet," he asked, just barely leaving her mouth to talk.

"Nope."

He kissed her again, but this time a little lighter, and lovingly.

"How about now?"

Quinn shook her head lightly, without breaking eye contact.

Ajax smiled and raised one large hand to her cheek, and slid it back to where his thumb was in front of her ear, and his long fingers were close to the back of her head. He slipped his free hand to the small of her back. He placed his lips barely on hers, burning her lips with his hot breath. He kissed her softly and slowly, pulling her in at her lower back. Quinn couldn't help but close her eyes, trying to fight the urge to crown him king. Ajax deepened the kiss, and he pulled her so close they were melting together. Quinn's legs were getting really unsteady, and she unwillingly made a sound she was trying to hide. Ajax stopped moving his mouth and kissed her on the nose, trying not to smile.

"How about now?"

It took Quinn a long moment before she could answer. Ajax knew she did this time, whether she said it or not, because he definitely did. His whole insides were a jittering mess of emotions and hormones.

"Regret isn't the word I'd use," she said, almost laughing at her silly self.

Ajax laughed at her unknowing expression, and kissed her again, but not as passionately this time; they both could use this time to cool off and regain their footing. Literally.

Quinn left the kiss first, leaning up against his chest, in a hug. "I'm gonna head home."

"Okay, Babe," Ajax said, planting a small peck on her lips, cheeks and forehead.

Chapter 43

"Good morning, Mom," Quinn sang, entering the kitchen the next Friday morning.

Her mom was standing in front of the coffee maker. She turned around, and handed Quinn a cup of coffee, and then sat down at the kitchen table.

"You hungry, Baby?"

Quinn shook her head, while blowing lightly on the top of her coffee. "No, Ma, but thank you. Wanna do some gardening today?" Quinn asked, smiling.

"Don't you have a dance to get ready for?" Quinn's mom asked, raising a brow.

"Seriously, Mom, it doesn't even start till 7:30."

Quinn's mom stood up, walked over to the counter, picked something up, turned, and handed it to Quinn. It was two time slots for getting nails done.

"Really, Mom? It's a dance; I'm not in high school anymore."

Her mom looked at her with a smile; happy lines surrounded her eyes.

"Actually, Mom, that'd be extremely awesome. Thank you."

Quinn and her mom sat side by side in the pedicure seats after their nails were done. The chairs they ended up in were delightfully soft. The smell was less harsh in this room. It smelled of lavender and other beautiful scents. Her mom sat back, with her eyes closed, and a soft smile creasing her soft, full lips. She looked so relaxed.

"Dear girl, why didn't we start doing these years ago?"

Quinn turned her resting head toward her mom. "'Cause we thought it was a waste," Quinn giggled. "We were totally wrong," she added.

"Yeah, we were," her mom lazily responded.

"Oh, yeah," Quinn said, enjoying the foot massage, which was taking place.

Quinn was resting in front of her mirror, in nothing but a robe, with her washed hair up in a towel, when he phone buzzed in front of her. A text from Ajax glowed brightly on her screen.

> *Hey, I'll pick you up about 7:20. I know we aren't supposed to go together, but we can drive there together. I'll see ya soon. Save me a dance. Xoxo.*

Quinn smiled, and typed:

Okay, sounds good.   I'll save you a dance. Xoxo.

At home, Quinn opened the makeup kit she'd got on the way home from the store. All her other makeup was old, and hadn't been used since her senior year. She took a small dab of cover-up, and blended it over her face. She opened the palette of eye shadow, and put dark brown in the creases of her eyelids, and then blended a bronze color over the rest of her lids; she added a little white to the corners and upper lids of her eyes. Lightly applying black eyeliner the outer parts of her water lines, she finished up with no-smear, light bronze, twelve-hour-wear lipstick. She sat for a moment, letting everything dry, and then added a light mist of some finishing spray her mother gave her. She looked at herself and smiled.

Quinn's mom arranged Quinn's hair into a half up-do. Most of her hair was in a controlled, messy bun, with locks falling around her face. Her mom added mini hair claws, with white angel wing and little, dangling diamonds, and bronze crosses, throughout the crown of her head. When her mom finished with her hair, Quinn put on her dress and shoes in the bathroom. When she came out, her mother gasped, and put her hand over her mouth.

"Oh, Baby, you look stunning!"

Quinn smiled, and gave her mom a hug. "Aw, thank you, Mama, and thanks for helping."

Her mom hugged her again. "Oh, you're so welcome, sweet girl."

The doorbell rang at 7:17. Quinn's mom disappeared, as Quinn went to answer the door. Quinn opened the door to a very well-dressed, handsome man standing there.

"Wow," Quinn smiled. "You look great," she added.

Ajax stepped in, and grinned. "You are … you look…" Ajax cleared his throat. "Breathtaking."

Quinn blushed, and froze.

"Hey, take the compliment. You're stunning every day, but your glow burns bright tonight," Ajax said, stepping in, and giving her a kiss.

"Thank you," she whispered, because her true voice seemed to have vanished.

"Hey, guys, can I get a picture before you head off? I know it's not the prom, but please, indulge me," her mom said, walking down the hall.

"Of course. Could you take one of just Quinn, too? I want one," Ajax said, smiling.

Quinn's mom called Ajax's mom to come over. They took pictures of Quinn and Ajax, separately and together. Then, each mom took pictures of the other with their children. Quinn's mom even got pictures when they didn't know they were being taken.

It was after 7:30 when they finally left the house. Ajax and Quinn drove together, holding hands over the divider. The ride was short, and filled with contented silence, but they gazed and smile at each other often. When they reached the hall, Ajax let Quinn out at the door. He said he would park, and then meet her inside in about thirty minutes, after they mingled, as Father David had asked. When Quinn entered the hall, the music was loud, but not blaring, as it would be at a school dance. The place wasn't extremely packed, but they did have a full house. The decorations were beautiful. The ceiling was blackened, with twinkling star light, made to look like the stars were falling, and clouds were brightly illuminated by a fake moon above. The lighting was dim, but just enough to set the mood, without letting the guests trip over each other. On the right side of the hall, tables were set up, with finger food. Quinn walked over, and poured herself some punch, which sat in the center of the table, which was covered with sweets. On the other end was a coffee bar.

"The guys did an awesome job," she thought.

Quinn smiled, and waved at Father David, who quickly crossed the room to greet her.

"You look very heavenly tonight, Quinn."

"Thank you," Quinn said, smiling.

"Where's Ajax?" Father David asked, looking around.

"He was parking the car about five minutes ago, so he should be around here somewhere. The way he dresses up, Father David, I wouldn't doubt he's beating girls off with a stick," Quinn said, smiling.

Father David laughed at Quinn's remark.

As Father David was about to say something, a slow song started playing, and a guy from Quinn's senior class walked up; he asked her to dance.

Quinn looked at Father David, a little nervously.

Father David smiled and nodded at her, encouraging her to accept.

"Yeah. Sure," Quinn agreed.

"Quinn, right?" the guy asked, as he led the dance.

"Yeah," Quinn agreed.

"I'm Andy Marks. I think we only had a few classes together, throughout high school."

Quinn nodded. She remembered him, but, like he said, they didn't cross paths often.

"So, Andy, what've you been up to since graduation?"

Andy let go of her waist, and twirled her once under his arm.

"I'm working for my dad, as his assistant, in his office. I'm also taking business classes, in the evenings. So, one day, I can take over for him."

Quinn smiled, but didn't know how to respond.

"So, what're you doing now?" Andy asked.

"I continued working at the factory, but full time, and not in the office."

Andy nodded. "Is that enough for you?"

"Ask me in a few years, Andy."

Andy smiled, and twirled her out again.

About 15 feet away, a sparkling set of eyes caught her attention. Ajax was staring at her, with a soft smile playing on his lips. He seemed to have found Dotty, a girl on the cheer team. Not stuck up at all, but very bubbly, she loved everyone. Quinn could see her chatting away, and Ajax looked amused. When the dance finally ended, Quinn thanked Andy for the dance, and tried to move from the floor, before another song started, but wasn't fast enough. Just as she reached the end of the dance floor, a guy she didn't recognize, a little older, asked her to dance. Quinn accepted, but refused to go any further into the crowd than where she was already standing.

When that dance finished, she rushed off the floor, and over to the junk food, where she snagged herself a cookie, as the music pick up its beat. Quinn's feet were already starting to hurt. After finishing her cookie, she found an empty table, which was littered with plastic cups and paper plates, and sat down to rest her feet.

Quinn scanned the dance floor, watching people dance to a song with a fast beat. She spotted Ajax, talking to Father David, in the corner, before being dragged away to the dance floor by a couple of younger girls. Quinn laughed at how demanding girls acted out of excitement. Quinn sat and nibbled her cookie. When the song ended, the D.J. made a couple of announcements, and cracked some jokes, before returning to the music. This time, it was a line dance of some sort.

"Hey, what're you doing?"

Quinn looked up to see Ajax, who found a chair at the other side of the table, with a water bottle.

"Resting my feet," she said, smiling. "And making small talk," she added.

Ajax laughed, and used a napkin to wipe his brow.

Ajax noticed Quinn's smile fade, and looked behind him, in the direction she was looking. Coming up right behind him was Katie.

"Hey," she said sweetly.

Quinn gave a stiff smile.

Katie was wearing a dress that was cut a couple of inches above the knee. The black dress was covered with red sequins, which made the light bounce around her. She wore a pair of eight inch heels, which set off her dress.

"You look very nice," Quinn surprised herself by saying.

Katie raised a brow, and smiled her signature Katie smile. "Thanks."

Just then, a slow song came on.

"I requested this song; it's so my fave," she squealed. "Dance with me?" she asked Ajax.

Ajax looked at Quinn. Quinn smiled, and nodded with no regrets.

Quinn tried not to watch, but she found it kind of hard. Katie, no matter how many times Ajax repositioned them, kept putting her face into his neck. Quinn wondered whether he was uncomfortable, because Quinn was watching, or because of the behavior Katie was exhibiting. Either way, Quinn was a little uncomfortable. When the dance ended, Katie kissed him. Even though Quinn watched him pull away and shake a finger at her, Quinn felt deeply bothered now.

Even after Ajax chewed her out, Katie still walk away smiling.

Before Ajax turned, and walked back toward the table, Quinn looked down at her plate. She wasn't upset with him; she wanted to cool down, before he could read her face.

"Hey, I'm sorry," Ajax said, kneeling at her side.

Quinn smiled and shook it off.

"I'm so not gonna get angry every times someone shows interest in you. That'd turn me into a raving crazy person," she said, winking.

Ajax opened his mouth to say something, but a blast of loud music interrupted him. He leaned over, and spoke in her ear. "Kick those shoes off, and dance with me."

Quinn shook her head vigorously, and mouthed, "To this? I can't."

Ajax pretended not to hear her, and slid her shoes off for her. He looked up, and grinned as he took her hand, and dragged her to the dance floor in a half run. Once there, he spun her until she was dizzy, and fell into to him. Quinn couldn't help but laugh at herself. She looked up at Ajax, flashing a toothy grin. He kissed her nose, and led her around the dance floor. He was pretty good at dancing, even though he was just goofing off to have fun. Quinn, on the other hand, just let him lead, because she had no idea what she was doing.

The music stopped short, and a slow song started. Quinn smiled.

"I love this song."

Ajax pulled her close, and leaned into her ear. "Mmm. *Unchained Melody.*"

With her hand in his, he raised it to his heart, and wrapped his free arm around her lower back. He moved, and her body just went with him. They were so close, she could feel his heartbeat. She took her arm, slid it up, and rested it on his bicep. Ajax smiled, and kissed her forehead. Quinn laid her cheek on his chest. His scent was pleasing, and his glow was illuminating. She was very content and relaxed. When the song ended, Ajax let her loose, kissed her lips sweetly, and led her off the dance floor, down the closed-off hallway.

"What're we doing in here?" Quinn asked.

Ajax leaned up against the wall, and smiled. "I got something for you."

Ajax reached into his pants pocket, and pulled out a plain, black, cardboard sleeve; he handed it to her. Quinn glanced at it, and then back up at him. She slowly slid a glossy picture out of the sleeve, and turned it over. It was a picture of

Ajax, sitting on the grass, when he was almost nine, and behind him stood a baby, maybe just over one, pulling herself up against his shoulders.

Quinn looked questioningly up at him. "Is this us?"

Ajax nodded and stepped forward. "Look at the parked cars behind us on the street. You see the motorcycle parked behind that old black car?"

Quinn nodded.

"Look at that man in the background, about to mount the bike."

"That can't be. It's not possible," Quinn gasped.

Ajax laughed.

"Of all the people saying it's impossible. You're stalked by a demon, or, who knows, maybe the devil himself, but that can't be Father David?"

"Oh, wow, he looks the same. Maybe a few years older, but that's it," Quinn said, still looking at the picture.

Ajax wrapped his arms around her from behind.

"I've been mulling on this for a few weeks. He shows up, days before my father takes me from my mother. He watches over you, even before he becomes a priest. I bet you can find him in other photos, as well. Then, he hasn't doubted anything you've told him about your dream," Ajax said, and kissed her cheek. "I think he's your personal angel, who's been trying to protect you from your own personal demons," Ajax added.

Quinn leaned up against Ajax, and slipped the picture back into the sleeve. "He's been here as a priest since the start of tenth grade. He was at our house at least two Sundays of the month, every holiday, birthday, BBQ, and even my graduation. He was pretty much there the same way my dad would have been."

Quinn fell silent.

"You alright?" Ajax asked, moving around to face her.

"Yeah, I think so," she said. Quinn smiled at Ajax. "Thank you."

Ajax kissed her lips, led her out of the hall, and back to the dance.

As they returned to the dance floor, Father David walked briskly toward them. "We spotted your father's men in town," Father Davis said, as he approached.

Ajax spat a curse word, and ran his hand through his hair. "Father David, can Quinn use your car?"

Father David nodded his head, and handed her the keys from his pocket. "You remember what to do." Father David said to Ajax, before walking away.

"What's he talking about, Ajax?"

Ajax turned to her, and took her hand. "I need you to take Father David's SUV, hit the highway, and head to the cabin."

Quinn narrowed her eyes, and her breathing started to pick up. "Why? You need to come, too.

I'm not going anywhere without you. I've seen what happens, Ajax."

Ajax shushed her. "Listen, I'll be following not far behind. It's just to throw them off."

A tear escaped Quinn's eye, and she brushed it away. "You promise?"

Ajax smiled. "I promise, Baby. Now, go, grab your stuff. I'll meet you in the back alley. I'll get the car started," Ajax said, running toward the back door.

Quinn grabbed her stuff off the table, and, waiting for her inside the back door, was Father David. Quinn hugged him tightly, and whispered, "I know. Thank you for everything."

Father David squeezed her tightly. "I want you to come back. Sometimes, fate isn't everything you think. We have ways of changing it. Just come home."

Quinn let go, and headed out the back door. "Did he say what I think he did?" she thought.

Ajax was waiting for her, with the driver's door open. "Don't stop; I'll be there no later than a half hour after you."

Quinn nodded, still a little upset, or scared, to say much, and slipped into the driver's seat. Ajax leaned in, and kissed her, so long that it left her breathless. He put his hands on her face, and smiled. "I love you. You know that, right?"

Quinn nodded, and a tear slipped from under her lids. "I love you, too," she choked out, with a sob.

"No crying, okay? I'm right behind you."

Ajax kissed her again, and walked away.

Quin put her foot on the gas, and sped off, in the direction of her fate.

Chapter 45

Quinn sped down the highway, quite possibly faster than she should have. The highway heading north was empty at one in the morning. She reached into the passenger's seat, and opened a bottle of water, which Father David must have left. It was warm, but helped cure her dry mouth. About a half hour later, she was driving down the bumpy, dirt road, which led to the cabin. When she pulled up, the whole place was dark, except for a little light from the moon, reflecting off the lake.

Quinn unbuckled herself, reached into her handbag for her phone, and sent Ajax a text, letting him know she'd made it. She shoved it back into her bag, and climbed out of the SUV. She carefully walked up the porch steps to the front door, and unlocked the door. When she walked in, it was dark. She reached for the light switch, and someone grabbed her arm, forcefully. Quinn tossed her bag down, and started whaling on the unseen person, who had hold of her arm. Suddenly, the light came on, blinding her, and a sharp pain hit the side of her face. The last thing she remembers was falling backwards.

Quinn knew she was dreaming. Everything surrounding her was hazy, and the colors were dim. She hid behind a tree, and heard a commotion in the distance. There was no sound or sight of wildlife. After a few minutes of waiting, she saw Ajax running through the clearing, a large, bald man chasing him. Quinn's dream took over, and she stepped out from behind the tree, as the man stopped to aim at Ajax. She pulled her gun, aimed, and shot her target. The bald man dropped almost instantly. When Ajax reached her, she carefully dropped the gun, and jumped into his arms, crying. Quinn saw more, but she knew what was going to happen, so she closed her eyes tightly, and willed herself awake.

When she opened her eyes, she was in the cabin, on the floor of the bedroom she and Ajax shared, the last time they were hiding out there.

Quinn moaned, and spit out the taste of blood in her mouth. She pulled herself to her feet, and went into the bathroom; she rinsed out her mouth, and cleaned whatever dried blood was on her face. She left the restroom. The nightstand clock read two in the morning.

"Ajax should be here by now," she thought.

Quinn went to the door. It was locked, or blocked, from the other side. There was no sound coming from the cabin, on the other side of the door. She beat on it for a while, but the door didn't budge, and no one came to shut her up. Quinn looked around the room, and her eyes landed on the closet.

Quinn smiled to herself, as she walked over, and climbed the shelves of the closet, until she reached the top cupboards. She reached far inside, and grabbed her father's Smith and Wesson, which she'd left there, due to her dreams. After bringing it down, she lay on the floor next to the bed they hadn't used, and squirmed half of her body under the bed. She reached around, until she felt a box tucked under the frame of the bed: the ammunition. She loaded the chamber, and made sure the safety was on.

When Quinn stood back up, she laid the gun on the dresser, next to the window, grabbed the smallest night stand in the room, and threw it at the window as hard as she could, shattering the window. She used a hand towel to dust the broken glass from the windowsill. She kicked her heels off, and climbed out of the window, onto the deck, which went all the way around the cabin; she reached back through the window, and grabbed the gun. She didn't want to go all the way around the house to the stairs, so she took the jump onto the ground, and made it, rolling a little at landing. Quinn stood there, and closed her eyes, looking for some direction from Michael. A few minutes later, she got a quick vision of Ajax, running through the woods toward the cabin, coming from the direction of Adam and Eve's. When the vision cleared, she took off running. She felt a timer in her gut, and, at the moment, time didn't seem to be on her side. She tried to stick to the narrow trails, but they weren't always running the direction she needed to go. After about 15 minutes of running, she stopped for a quick breather, and to check on her cut-up feet. When her breathing slowed, she closed her eyes again, and waited. It took a little longer, this time, but the vision came through. She headed in the direction that was given to her.

After another hour of off and on running, she had to stop. She put her back to a tree, and slid down. Her chest ached, and her feet hurt something horrible. Her eyes drifted closed, and the pain disappeared.

When her eyes opened again, the sun was just rising, and everything looked hazy, just like in her dream, but, this time, she was awake. She listened, and looked around. There was no sign or sound of chirping birds, or any scurrying wildlife. She knew the dreadful time was drawing near. She pulled the gun out from behind her, turned off the safety, and waited.

While she waited, she prayed. "Dear God, grant me a clear mind and a pure heart. Give me the strength and bravery to protect. Put your hand on Ajax, and help protect him from harm."

Quinn chanted the prayer over and over, until she thought she heard rustling sounds from aways away.

"I'm not ready," she whispered.

She broke out into a cold sweat, and her hands started shaking. Quinn closed her eyes, and took a deep breath, allowing a heavenly warmth to come over her. Her body stopped shaking, and her hearing was clear. She could hear the light snapping of twigs, from behind her, letting her know they were coming, but were still a couple of minutes away. Quinn sat there, and listened, with her eyes closed, and her senses alert.

After a couple of minutes, the snapping and stomping of feet became clearer and closer. Quinn stood up, and made sure she couldn't be seen. She peeked around the tree, to see Ajax's form heading in her direction, but she stayed in the cover of the trees, until she saw the other body, a big, bald man, coming up from behind. Quinn then stepped out from behind her tree, and everything went into slow motion. She held the gun up, put herself in perfect form, and waited for a clear shot. When life shifted back out of slow motion, the bald man was in her sights. She aimed, breathed, and then she fired. She watched, as the man dropped, almost instantly, to the ground. Quinn waited a moment, before lowering the gun, and putting it on the grass.

Quinn ran to Ajax, jumped into his arms, and held him as tightly as she could. He was a dirty, sweaty mess, but that didn't deter her at all. She held him for a moment longer, before letting him go.

"You alright?" she asked, stepping back, her eyes darting around, looking for any visible injuries.

"Don't worry about me. Are you okay?" he asked, rubbing his thumb along her bruised lower lip.

Quinn nodded and smiled, as tears streamed down her face. "I saw you die so many times."

Ajax pulled her face against his chest, and held her there. Quinn closed her eyes, and a vision came across her thoughts. Her eyes shot open, and a sad smile crossed her face.

Quinn looked up, and smiled at him.

"Do you remember kissing me the other day, after lunch, in front of the hall?"

Ajax nodded.

"Do you remember the last kiss you gave me?"

Ajax smiled. Yeah, I don't think that'd be easy to forget."

"Kiss me like that. Right here. Right now."

Ajax grabbed hold of her hip, and slid his hand from it to the small of her back; he pulled her close, his face now serious, and just as handsome as ever. He ran his fingertips from her fingertips, up the outside of her arm, to her cheek, and slid it back, behind her head, his thumb softly rubbing the spot in front of her ear. Ajax dipped his head, and kissed her. When it started becoming passionate, his eyes finally closed, and so did hers, in pleasure.

Then, she felt it. The sharp point of a knife, painfully puncturing her back. She felt it turn, ripping her insides, and she gasped loudly in pain, as it was pulled out. Their eyes flew open. Ajax's face showed horror, as he watched Dantanian disappear into a black mist.

Quinn gasped again, as Ajax pulled her close, and look down at her back.

"No. No. No!" he whispered, in sheer panic and shock, and then he started shaking. The blood was seeping quickly through her bronze dress.

The pain was minimal, but Quinn felt herself falling, just not to the ground.

"Hey, it's okay. I did it," she said, in a slow, struggling whisper.

Ajax held her tighter in his arms.   Tears streamed down his face.   Quinn wiped away a tear, and smiled.

"You'll be okay. Everything'll be okay now," she said, quietly, with a faint smile.   She also mumbled something that sounded like "letters in my night stand."

"You've gotta stay with me, Quinn! Stay with me!   Please," Ajax pleaded, as he watched the color drain from her face with every staggered breath she took.

Quinn mouthed, "I love you," and, slowly, her eyes closed.

"I love you more," Ajax said, kissing her forehead, as she slowly faded away.

Chapter 46

Dearest Ajax,

If you're reading this, it means I couldn't find another way to save you from the path that was swayed by evil. I've known all along what I needed to do. I'm the only one to blame for your pain, and the grief you're going through right now, and I'm sorry you have to feel this way, but I'm not sorry about my choice. The pain you feel will ease, with time, and when it does, I have a feeling Father David can fill you in on what I can't. The only thing I know is that you're meant to fulfill your destiny, and what you'll do will have a huge impact on the human world. You're important, and needed here.

I want you to know that you meant everything to me, and I love you so much. I may not be physically with you, but believe me when I say I don't plan on leaving your side, till I know you're okay. Who knows, maybe we'll meet again, someday, and finish our journey, which we didn't have time for.

XoXo Quinn Xoxo.

Chapter 47

Dear Father David,

You're the man who helped me find faith when I needed it most.   If you get this letter, it means I'm now walking with God, and it was the path I chose.   I know you understand death, more than anyone else, but there'll be people who need your help adjusting.   Could you please look after Mom, 'cause this'll be hard for her to get through alone.

Please give Ajax my necklace, and tell him I wanted him to wear it.   Between you and me, it's for his safety.   We all know how his path can still be altered, as it was before.

Thank you for everything, Father David.

Quinn

To My Readers

Thank you for purchasing and reading my novel, *Quinn's Faith*. If you enjoyed it, please feel free to leave a review on Amazon, Goodreads, or both!

You can also connect with me on social media. To find me on Facebook, just search 'Author Diane Garner'. From there, you can find links to my profiles on Goodreads and Amazon Author Page.

More Books
by Diane Garner

- Poems (2018)

About the Author

 Diane Garner lives in southeast Michigan with her husband and two young daughters. She grew up in Gaylord, Michigan, with her mom and brother. She moved to the Detroit area in her late teens to be with the man she now calls her husband; they have been married for 15 years. Diane's writing gives her a temporary escape from reality, and a chance to explore the fantasies created by her active imagination. She enjoys nothing more than curling up when the house is quiet with her laptop, 80-pound dog, very disruptive cat, and a steaming cup of coffee, and letting her stories write themselves.

Check out these books by Debbie Barry on her
Amazon Author Page:

https://www.amazon.com/author/debbiebarry